World War II

AMERICAN MERCHANT MARINE AND ARMED GUARD VETERANS

Drawn by Oswald Brett, able Seaman, RMS QUEEN ELIZABETH
Life Member, Project Liberty Ship

UNITED STATES MERCHANT MARINE, LIBERTY SHIPS AND Z-MEN

THIS IS A HISTORICAL STUDY OF THE WWII U.S. MERCHANT MARINE, ONE PARTICULAR SHIP (LIBERTY) AND THE MEN (Z-MEN AND GUNNERS) WHO MANNED THE MERCHANT FLEET? THIS PERIOD OF TURMOIL SAW THE U.S. GOING FROM, COMPARATIVELY SPEAKING, A VERY POOR MERCHANT MARINE TO THE WORLD'S GREATEST SHIPPING POWER—WITH ALL VOLUNTEER PERSONNEL. THESE Z-MEN ARE QUITE POSSIBLY THE LARGEST COLLECTION OF CRAZY, WILD, YOUNG MEN DOING A SERIOUS JOB THAT WAS EVER ASSEMBLED.

THIS STUDY WAS ORIGINALLY PRESENTED AS A DISSERTATION FOR A DOCTOR OF PHILOSOPHY DEGREE. THE READER WILL FIND THE PRESENTATION IN A PRESENT TENSE FORM.

IT IS THE FERVENT DESIRE OF THE AUTHOR THAT A GENERAL KNOWLEDGE OF THE WWII U.S. MERCHANT MARINE AND THE Z-MEN AND GUNNERS WILL BE THE RESULT OF THIS PRESENTATION.

SPECIAL THANKS GO TO EDWARD G. DIERKES, JACK G. GROTHE, AND JOHN LUDWIG. THESE OLD Z-MEN GAVE INVALUABLE FACTUAL ASSISTANCE THAT IS GREATLY APPRECIATED. A VERY SPECIAL THANKS ALSO GOES TO THE ARTIST, THOMAS L. WEHMER FOR THE COVER WHICH WAS ADAPTED FROM HIS WATER COLOR PAINTING.

THIS BOOK COULD NOT HAVE BEEN COMPLETED WITHOUT THE ASSISTANCE OF MY WIFE, DOROTHY. HER ONLY REWARD IS THE KNOWLEDGE SHE ACQUIRED THROUGH MANY HOURS OF ASSISTING IN THE PREPARATION OF THE FINISHED PRODUCT. HER GENERAL KNOWLEDGE OF THE U.S. MERCHANT MARINE NOW EQUALS THAT OF THE AVERAGE Z-MAN.

GEORGE E. WARD. JR..

A.A. A.A.S. B.S. M.S. PHD

THIS BOOK IS DEDICATED TO ALL THE BRAVE Z-MEN WHO VOLUNTARILY AND COURAGEOUSLY SERVED THIS GREAT COUNTRY IN ITS TIME OF GREAT NEED.

© Copyright 2007 George E. Ward, Jr.
All rights reserved. No part of this publication may be reproduced, stored in a retrieval system, or transmitted, in any form or by any means, electronic, mechanical, photocopying, recording, or otherwise, without the written prior permission of the author.

Note for Librarians: A cataloguing record for this book is available from Library and Archives Canada at www.collectionscanada.ca/amicus/index-e.html
ISBN 1-4251-1982-4

Printed in Victoria, BC, Canada. Printed on paper with minimum 30% recycled fibre. Trafford's print shop runs on "green energy" from solar, wind and other environmentally-friendly power sources.

Offices in Canada, USA, Ireland and UK

Book sales for North America and international:
Trafford Publishing, 6E–2333 Government St.,
Victoria, BC V8T 4P4 CANADA
phone 250 383 6864 (toll-free 1 888 232 4444)
fax 250 383 6804; email to orders@trafford.com
Book sales in Europe:
Trafford Publishing (UK) Limited, 9 Park End Street, 2nd Floor
Oxford, UK OX1 1HH UNITED KINGDOM
phone +44 (0)1865 722 113 (local rate 0845 230 9601)
facsimile +44 (0)1865 722 868; info.uk@trafford.com
Order online at:
trafford.com/07-0387

10 9 8 7 6 5 4 3

PREFACE

The U.S. Merchant Marine is an essential and very important part in gaining the victory in WW II. Unfortunately very few Americans know the role played by the Merchant Marine—its ships and the Seamen who man them. This historical study portrays one ship—The Liberty and the Z-Men of the Merchant Marine. It is the purpose of this report to enlighten young American men and women as to the importance of this phase of the U.S Merchant Marine in WW II.

Chapter 1 presents the shipping problems that the U.S.A. faced prior to WW II. Woefully unprepared the U.S. awakens and faces the difficult task ahead. Planning and setting up the machinery for one of the biggest management problems the world has ever confronted.

Chapter 2 is a review of the literature utilized in the presentation of the Merchant Marine prior to, during, and following WW II. Information has been collected from books, speeches, the Internet, articles, and individuals –most of whom were there. Statistics are from a number of sources both government and private.

Chapter 3 indicates the nautical problems when Pearl Harbor is attacked by the Japanese and the U.S. goes to war. A problem most Americans both then and now are unaware of is that the U.S. must build ships faster than the enemy can sink them. How this tremendous task is confronted and how it is to be accomplished is presented.

Chapter 4 deals with WW II and how the Merchant Marine copes with these problems. Shipbuilding, recruitment, and training of ship personnel (Z-Men) and many of the problems faced and the solutions found in defeating a tough enemy. The problems the U.S. Maritime Service trainee encounters, as he becomes a Z-Man on a ship that may be torpedoed, bombed, or hit by a mine are stated. The Z-Man may go on the Murmansk Run, may have to face a kamikaze, may be on one of the Liberties that breaks in half, or he may have an uneventful trip. Whatever problems the individuals face the overall goal of victory is finally reached.

Chapter 5 relates the problems the Z-Man faces after WW II. There is a long fight to obtain veteran status. All those ships remaining must be disposed of. Some are still working although they are resting on the bottom of the sea as fish reefs. Finally only two remain intact. Those interested can go aboard these grand, old ships and relive a little history of the greatest Merchant Fleet ever assembled—The United States Merchant Marine.

TABLE OF CONTENTS

CHAPTER 1

PRE-WWII U.S. MERCHANT MARINE

INTRODUCTION

    World in Turmoil..1

PROBLEM.

    USMM Is Inadequate ....………………………....4

IMPORTANCE OF THIS STUDY

    USMM Must Be Improved..4

SCOPE OF STUDY

    Focus On One Ship................................…...........................4

    Selection of a Cargo Ship—The Liberty........………….......4

    What Corporations Can Do The Job....................….......5

RATIONALE

    Selection of Shipbuilders..6

    Recruitment and Training of Employees.............................7

    Recruitment and Training of Ship Personnel........................7

DEFINITION OF TERMS

    Required for Seamen...8

    Desirable for Laymen...8

OVERVIEW OF STUDY

       Instituting Proper Solution Programs..........................14

CHAPTER 2

REVIEW LITERATURE..17

CHAPTER 3

METHODOLOGY AND APPROACH..25

       The U.S. Goes to War..25

       Shipbuilding in Full Progress..26

       Recruitment in Full Progress...27

       Summary.... The U.S A. Is Meeting The Task............36

CHAPTER 4

The WW II Years...37

       Way Behind but catching up..............................37

       U.S. Maritime Service to U.S. Merchant Marine........43

       Liberty Ship Duty...50

       Bob Hope's Christmas Broadcast..........................62

       A New Record..71

       Naval Disaster and Poison Gas............................75

       United Seamen's Service.....................................86

       Gallant Ships...87

       The Lost Convoy..96

Japanese Atrocities—Americans Beheaded	100
Shipboard Problems	102
Project Ivory Soap	116
Merchant Medals and Ribbons	118
D-Day Normandy Invasion	122
Victory in Europe	130

CHAPTER 5

POST WORLD WAR II MERCHANT MARINE	141
The Liberty Ship	141
The Z-Men Go Home	143
Seamen's Pay	144
Z-Men Killed	148
Military Leaders Comments	152
Z-Men Fight for Status	156
Artificial Fish Reefs	170
Last of the Liberties	172
The Final Two Liberties	173
U.S. Merchant Marine in the 21st Century	179
Sea Stories	182
Conclusion	194

BIBLIOGRAPHY

APPENDICES

CHAPTER 1

INTRODUCTION

WORLD IN TURMOIL

PRE WWII UNITED STATES MERCHANT MARINE

The year is 1940 and the world is again in turmoil. The Japanese have seized a number of islands in the Pacific and have invaded China. The Axis, a group composed of Fascist and pro-Fascist nations in Europe under the leadership of Adolph Hitler and Germany, are marching across Europe and North Africa. The U.S.A. always considers itself somewhat invulnerable with the Pacific and Atlantic Oceans as buffers to the east and west. Although there are some anti-war isolationists wanting the U.S.A. to remain neutral, it has become apparent that this is not possible. Modern technology has shrunk the world creating a problem that must be confronted by the U.S.A. in the very near future.

PROBLEM

UNITED STATES MERCHANT MARINE IS INADEQUATE

The U.S.A. having dismantled the WWI war machine and just coming out of the Great Depression, realizes it is faced with the biggest management and administrative program in its history. Just one of the many very important phases is planning, building and organizing a modern Merchant Fleet with properly trained men capable of coping with an already formidable potential enemy.

Then on May 21, 1941 a German submarine sinks the S.S. Moor owned by a U.S. shipping company, The Robin Line. (U.S. Merchant Marine Turner Publisher 1993 p.10). The Moor, although clearly marked with U.S. flags, is sunk in a neutral zone in the South Atlantic. The U-Boat does surface and gives the crew some provisions before shelling the ship. Crewmembers spend 15 days in lifeboats before being picked up. As a result of this incident Congress authorizes that Merchant Ships be armed.

A review of the U.S Merchant Fleet shows that the few remaining cargo ships constructed in WWI are too slow at 10 – 15 knots (U.S. Merchant Marine Turner Publisher 1993 p.70). The concrete ships, referred to as "floating tombstones" by the Seamen, are too expensive to operate and are now obsolete.. (Floating Tombstones, http://unmuseum.mus.pa.us/concrete.html). Only a few wooden ships remain and they are soon retired. The small number of passenger, tanker and cargo ships available leaves no doubt that the U.S.A. is a second rate maritime power.

A total of less than 20,000 skilled shipbuilding workers is available. Only 102 ships are built in 1939-1940 (Weichert 2003). As world issues continue to heat up, a survey indicates to President Roosevelt that the American Merchant Fleet is very inadequate as the U.S. prepares for the coming conflict.

Up to this time large shipping companies privately own all Merchant Ships. These peacetime commercial trade conditions must be changed and all Merchant

Ships will have to come under the control of the United States government. More ships will be needed, and thousands of men will be required to man them.

The United States has a total of only 900 dry-cargo vessels of 6,700,000 dead weight tons and some 400 tankers of 5,150,000 dead weight tons. This total includes all the foreign vessels, which we have acquired by negotiation, requisition, and seizure from foreign countries. Not a solid foundation for entering a conflict.

In addition to gearing up our shipbuilding program, we still need thousands of seamen trained in, not only seafaring practices, but also seamen who are skilled in the use of cannons and machine guns. Older retired seamen who are physically fit are encouraged to come back to sea. Seamen who have taken jobs on land are enticed back. Additionally a system must be devised to recruit and train new seamen.

The Selective Training and Service Act of 1940 is signed by President Roosevelt and is the first draft in peacetime for the United States. (History of the Draft, en.wikipedia.org/wiki selective-service act). Unfortunately for the U.S. Merchant Marine, selective service does not include provisions to draft seamen. Other services are also having problems and will soon need many more men, training facilities, equipment etc. The first peacetime draftees are training with wooden guns. Every facet of our war machine is playing "catch-up". Many of the draftees will complete their twelve months only to be called back up later.

IMPORTANCE OF THIS STUDY

UNITED STATES MERCHANT MARINE MUST BE IMPROVED

The importance of the problem is very clear. After careful study the United States needs to formulate plans and implement programs and work to a successful conclusion. It is very simple—we produce or we do not survive as a nation. No one thinks it is an easy task, as we are facing an enemy on several fronts who has been preparing for years. We are now faced with the biggest challenge in almost a century.

SCOPE OF STUDY

FOCUS ON ONE SHIP

The scope of this study is to focus on one ship, The Liberty, and the personnel to man her. The Merchant Marine Act of 1936 has revived the art of shipbuilding and it is now time to gear up a war program. The ship destined to be the workhorse of American War Shipping is a modified British "ocean" ship. In early 1941 Admiral Emory S. Land, chairman of the United States Maritime Commission shows the British design to President Franklin Roosevelt, who agrees that this is the ship needed. A goal of 200 of these vessels to be constructed is now announced in February 1941. (Jaffee <u>The Liberty Ship From A To Z</u> 2004). The President describes the ships as "dreadful looking objects". These ships are soon to be called "The Ugly Ducklings". The first of these ships is christened The S.S. Patrick Henry. The inspiration from the words "Give me liberty or give me death" produces the ship's namesake. Hence we now have the "Liberty Ship".

The Liberty is in the category of "dry cargo ship, EC2-S-C-1 Type" This system of numbers and letters is used to classify ships by three groups. The E is emergency, C is cargo and 2 represents a length ranging from 400" to 450". The S stands for steam and the C1 indicates the ship design and modification.

Most Liberties are named for Americans who made some impact on United States history or life. Some are named for American Merchant Marine heroes from captains all the way down to Seamen. Over 100 are named for women and some are named for killed war correspondents. All ship names are for those deceased except one, The S.S. Francis O'Gara, who was thought to be dead. At the end of the war he is found in a Japanese prisoner of war camp.

Shipyards to build the Liberties and other ships are quickly built. Shipbuilding companies capable of constructing these ships are selected. Shipbuilding workers are hired and trained. Training camps to instruct new seamen are located. Training facilities and equipment are purchased and erected and/or installed. Training manuals are written and printed. Techniques are readied and instructors are prepared. Thousand of men are recruited for a wartime Merchant Marine. In short, this is an awesome job that is accomplished very quickly and efficiently!

RATIONALE

SELECTION OF SHIPBUILDERS

It is reasonable from the review of problems faced and requirements to be met that the best possible leaders and companies be selected and that is exactly what the government does.

In January 1941 contracts to build the Liberties are awarded to the Bethlehem-Fairfield Shipyard, Inc. in Baltimore and the Oregon Shipbuilding Corporation in Portland, Oregon. Shortly after this other shipyards are also under contract. Theses are Permanente Metals Corporation, California Shipbuilding Corporation, Delta Shipbuilding Company, J.A. Jones Construction Company, New England Shipbuilding Corporation, North Carolina Shipbuilding Company, Southeastern Shipbuilding Corporation, Todd Houston Shipbuilding Corporation, Kaiser Company, Alabama Dry-dock Company, Mariaship Corporation, St. John's River Shipbuilding Company and Walsh-Kaiser Company. (Jaffee, The Liberty Ships from A-Z 2004) In all fifteen shipbuilders are now actively working around the clock to put the Liberties to sea. (liberty E C 2 p.6a.)

RECRUITMENT OF SHIPBUILDING EMPLOYEES.

Now employees are hired and trained to build these ships. Workers come from everywhere. Many of them have never even seen a ship before. Due to the shortage of men, women are hired and trained. Most of them have never worked in any factory before. In fact, most of the women have never worked in

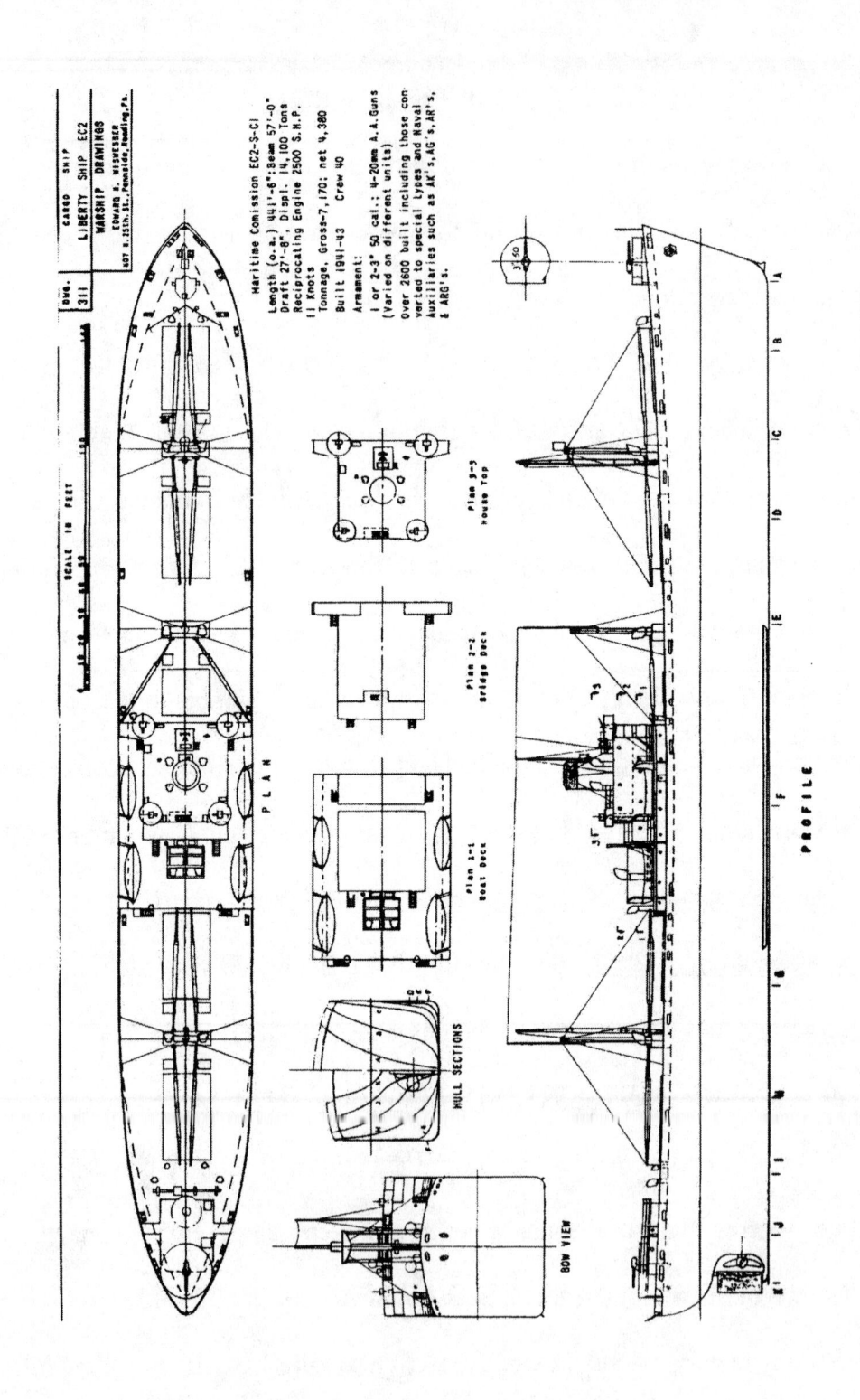

LIBERTY SHIP PROFILE

any job outside the home. They are simply housewives. "Rosie the Riveter" takes jobs that previously have been only man's domain. The women perform superbly.

RECRUITMENT OF SEAMEN

Only about 15,000 merchant seamen and officers have been sailing prior to WWII. Now a program must be initiated to mobilize, train and assign to ships a large number of recruits. The WSA (War Shipping Administration) to be authorized in 1942 will create the Recruitment and Manning Organization, which will be known as the "RMO", the Training Organization and the Maritime Labor Relations Organization.

Ex-merchant seamen are encouraged to return to sea. Many are reluctant to leave better paying, safer jobs. There is an effort to enroll C.C.C. (Civilian Conservation Corps) men. A commitment of one-year service is made by young men between the ages of 18 and 23.

The WSA Training Organization will provide men by three different divisions i.e. The United States Merchant Marine Academy at King's Point, New York, The United States Maritime Service and Officer Schools to train deck and engine room men.

DEFINITION OF TERMS

REQUIRED FOR RECRUITS—DESIRABLE FOR LAYMEN

A seaman on any merchant ship soon learns the nomenclature of the sea or suffers ridicule. Some of the more common nautical words are: (Boattalk 2005 www.boattalk.com/dictionsry/index.htm); (Cornell and Allan 1942)

Anchor: A chained heavy metal object when dropped catches on the bottom and holds the ship in place

Astern: Toward the ships back (rear) end

Batten Down: Secure hatch covers and tarps

Beam: The width (measurement) from port side to starboard side

Below: That part of the ship below the deck

Block: Wooden or metal housing that contains the pulleys

Boat: Never used in reference to the ship It is a small craft that can be carried on a ship

Bouy: Floating device that marks the channel, warns of dangerous area, aids in mooring

Cabin: Compartment (room) for officers or passengers

Capsize: Turn over

Cast Off: Take in lines and leave dock

Channel: Name given to narrow passage of water connecting two larger bodies of water. Body of water deep enough for safe passage of ships

Chart: Ship's navigation (2nd mate's job) map

Chock: Opening for passage of mooring lines or anchor

Cleat: Fixed steel device with two extensions used to secure lines

Coil: A line rolled up in a circle to prevent knotting

Compass: Device showing magnetic north

Current: Direction that water is moving

Cross Over The Bar: To die

Crow's Nest: High position on mast for lookouts

Dead Ahead: Direction straight forward

Dead Behind: Direction straight backward

Deck: Floor

Dock: Protected area where ship is moored. Often called a pier or wharf

Ease: Release pressure on line

Ebb Tide: Reflux of water. Low tide

Fast: One object that is firmly secured to another

Fathom: 6 feet length

Fender: Object placed on the side of ship to prevent damage when tied to dock or another ship. May be constructed of wood, tires, etc

Flare: Distress signal

Flying Bridge: Open deck above normal control room with similar controls used for greater visibility

Focscle: Crew's quarters (rooms)

Forward: Toward the ship's bow

Galley: Ship's kitchen

Gear: Refers to all equipment such as line, blocks and tackle

Gunwale: Upper edge of ship's sides

Gyro: Device that shows true north. Used by seaman steering ship

Harbor: A ship's safe anchorage

Hatch: Opening and area for storing cargo

Hawser: Heavy rope or line

Head: Toilet

Heading: Course or direction

Headway: Forward movement

Heaving Line: A light, flexible line with a heavy knot (monkey fist) on one end used to pass a hawser (line or rope) to dock when trying up

Helm: The steering wheel, which controls the rudder

Hold: Compartment or area for storing cargo

Hull: Ship's main body

Jettison: To cast overboard unwanted objects

Keel: The backbone of a ship—centerline fore and aft

Knot: 1. To tie two ropes together

2. Wound up rope forming a stopper

3. Nautical mile (6076.115 feet)

Life Preserver: Flotation device designed to keep individual afloat if ship is abandoned. Also called a life jacket.

Life Ring: Flotation device easily thrown to individual in water who is without a life preserver

Line: Rope or hawser

Log: A record of a ships daily activity

Mast: Steel poles used to support cargo booms. Also supports crows nest, signal lights and wireless antennas

Monkey Fist: Properly wound knot (approx. 4-5" in diameter on end of heaving line

Nautical Mile: 6076.115 feet or about 1/8 longer than a statue mile (5,280 ft)

Navigation: Science of conducting a ship from one point to another

Overboard: Over the ship's side into the sea

Painter: A line used for towing or hauling

Pier: Platform for docking ship to load or unload

Plimsoll Mark: Painted on each side of the ship to indicate the maximum level ship is to be loaded for different oceans and different seasons

Port: 1. A harbor

    2. Left side of ship

Propeller: Two or more blades that turn to propel the ship

Roll: Motion of ship leaning alternating to port (left) and starboard (right)

Rudder: A vertical plate at stern (back) that turns the ship

Running Lights: Lights required in peace time to indicate the ship's direction

Screw: Ship propeller

Scupper: Opening to allow water to run off

Scuttlebutt: 1. Drinking fountain

        2. Ship word for gossip, rumor, story, etc

Secure: To make fast

Shackle: U shaped connector with bolt on open end

Squall: Period of rain or wind

Square Knot: Used to tie same size lines

Starboard: Right side of ship

Stem: Front part of bow

Stern: Back or after part of ship

tow: To pack and store all line, equipment etc.

Swamp: To fill with water

Tackles: Blocks and line

Tide: Rise and fall of the sea

Topsides: Area on and above deck

Underway: Ship is in motion

Wake: Track following ship when underway

Wharf: Dock or pier

Winch: Device used in mooring, loading or unloading

If sailing boat terms are desired, Boattalk provides a glossary for that type of vessel.

OVERVIEW OF THE STUDY

INSTITUTION OF PROPER PROGRAMS

The problem is quite clear. The United States must prepare to go ahead at full speed.

For the ever approaching war to be won the U.S. Merchant Marine must be ready to deliver the troops, vehicles, weapons, ammunition and supplies to every area of the world where needed. The ship designated to be the workhorse has been selected and this ship - "The Liberty"- is now being constructed by 15 very capable ship building corporations-the most notable being Henry Kaiser.

Henry J. Kaiser meets with the British delegation in November 1940 to work on a contract with the U.S. for the construction of ships. He is asked, "Where are your shipyards?" Kaiser said, "These are our shipyards!" pointing to the mud flats with a gesture of his hand. ("The Mighty Liberties" S.S. Samuel Parker Newsletter January 1, 2006) The British needed the ships badly, but they wondered about this man who had never built a ship. At this time the German Luftwaffe (air force) is devastating the British cities and sea borne supplies are desperately needed. As it were the British did let the contract for 60 ships.

Kaiser emphasized speed and construction. Records are broken. Workers are hired. Then comes the problem of housing for all these men and women. Many sleep in shacks, under highway bridges and even in their cars. Local schools can't handle all of the children who accompany the parents. Unfortunately an unsavory element follows the workers and soon the local jails are filled to over-flowing. Kaiser sets up a good health program and workers use the 175-bed field hospital when needed.

Kings Point Academy in New York is now the equivalent of West Point and Annapolis. Young men selected for this academy are receiving the best naval education the country has ever provided. Two basic schools are now providing preliminary training in California at San Mateo and in the South at Pass Christian, Mississippi.

The United States Maritime Service has large training camps at Catalina Island, California, Sheep's Head Bay in New York and St. Petersburg, Florida. Men are recruited all over the United States, sworn in and sent by train to one of these training centers. There they are given the required injections, issued uniforms similar to those worn by the navy and instructed in all three departments i.e. deck, engine and steward much as in a naval boot camp. Heavy stress is centered on weaponry and lifeboat skills.

There are special schools to train deck and engine men with 14 months sea duty to become officers. After 4 months training they become mates and engineers.

After 5 weeks of basic training in the United States Maritime Service those selected to become pursers or radio operators receive instruction at Gallups Island, Mass. or Hoffman Island, New York.

The United States Merchant Marine is preparing to "DELIVER THE GOODS". This has always been its motto.

CHAPTER 2

REVIEW OF RELATED LITERATURE

Information on the Liberty Ship can be found in many sources such as "The American Legion Magazine" and newsletters published by different other veteran groups, such as the Navy Armed Guard-the Navy Gunners-assigned to U.S. Merchant ships to man the guns. The Navy League is one of the best organizations for factual information on the Navy, Marines, Coast Guard, and the Merchant Marine.

The American Merchant Seaman's Manual is of considerable interest to the layman and is an invaluable guide for the man or woman who decides to pursue a sea career. It has a nautical and commercial terms section in both English and Spanish. It contains chapters on the many facets of both deck and engine Seamen i.e. splicing, block and tackle, paint and painting, steering, handling small boats under oars and sails, navigation, weather, first aid, ship sanitation, a tanker man's guide, hose connections, pump valves, pressure gauges, etc. Most important is information on requirements and examination for lifeboat certificates.

There are a number of books written by persons who have been to sea. Some are works of fiction that still tell an interesting story based on some facts and some personal experiences. There are some books that document history. Captain Frank F. Farrar's A Ship Log Book is included in this study for it's all too often plimsoll violation portrayal. Many ships are overloaded in trying to deliver maximum cargo to the troops. Captain Farrar's account shows the fears and frustrations that can and do occur many times. Captain Farrar went to sea as a deck boy at age 16 and deciding that this was the life for him worked all the way up to captain. His book is a true account of sea ventures. This book is recommended to anyone desiring a close up of how sea life really is.

"Floating Tombstones" is included to show how inventive shipbuilders can be. Yes, there are ships made of concrete.

Bob Hope's 1944 Christmas message to seamen has to be repeated for the joy and good will it provides for all service men. It's also an opportunity to introduce the tag "Z Men". Bob Hope undoubtedly did more for all servicemen than any other Hollywood performer. He took his troup to WWII and every military action until his demise.

Three of Captain Jaffee's books are included. The first one <u>The Last Liberty</u> was published in 1993. It gives a brief history of the origin of the Liberty Ship and then relates the full story of the S.S. Jeremiah O'Brien from her first trip to her last trip in WWII and then to her rebirth in 1979. Every man who was a crewmember or gunner is listed along with photos that bring this Liberty to life.

The second book <u>S.S. Jeremiah O'Brien</u> traces the early days of this vessel and then gives a full account of her return to Normandy on the 50th Anniversary of D-Day in 1994. She was the only original vessel returning from 1944. Captain

Jaffee, a King's Point Merchant Marine Academy graduate, received his Master's License at age 26. He has devoted his life to the sea and the Merchant Marine related positions.

Captain Jaffee's third book The Liberty Ships From A-Z published in 2004 contains 722 pages. It gives a background on the United States situation prior to WWII and then tells of all the steps taken by the U.S. to prepare for war. It gives the full story on all the shipbuilding companies, the shipyards, shipyard men and women, the seamen and the ships complete with pictures Most important—every Liberty constructed is listed complete with a thumbnail sketch of the person the ship is named after, the shipbuilder, the date the ship was delivered and its final disposition. Also there is the story of the two Liberties in existence i.e. The S.S. Jeremiah O'Brien and the S.S. John W. Brown. If an individual has only one book on the Liberty ship, this should be it.

There is a wealth of information about The Merchant Marine and the Liberties on the Internet.

World War II Strange and Fascinating Facts by McCombs and Worth has little concerning The United States Merchant Marine, but it is one of the first widely published books that makes it known that one Liberty ship still remains intact. The book is highly recommended to WW II buffs.

Information from the S.I.U., its president, Mike Sacco, and the Paul Hall Center is presented in later chapters to bring the United States Merchant Marine into the 21st century. This can be very important for the young man and woman who might consider the sea as an exciting vocation. The pay is good, the job is interesting and the travel can't be beat.

"Monthly Pay Scale for Liberty Vessels" is included and additional comments for very valid reasons will follow. There is much controversy on the U.S. Merchant Seaman's pay. This chapter should provide an answer to the critics. One can learn the negative facts that are not known, or if known are not acknowledged by certain groups.

Merchant Marine emblems, medals, ribbons and charts will show what seamen receive for their service and the special citations for action beyond the call of duty. Ship citations are also included. These service recognitions are not very well known to the general public. For instance, how many people know that a combat ribbon is only awarded to a seaman if the ship he is on is damaged by the enemy? The ship just ahead can be sunk, but if the ship following is not hurt no combat ribbons are issued to the men on that ship. No star is authorized on the combat ribbon unless the ship goes down. When an old sea veteran has two or three stars on his combat ribbon, <u>he has been there</u>.

National Maritime Day Proclamation 2005 by President of the United States of America—George W. Bush 2005. This proclamation is made annually reminding the public that May 22nd is National Maritime Day.

Reminick in his <u>Nightmare in Bari</u> has to be included to let the reader know two things:

(1) Bari was the worst naval bombing raid since Pearl Harbor. It took just 30 minutes, but Bari, Italy saw 18 allied ships sunk. (Including 5 Liberties) Not only were many servicemen killed but there was also a heavy toll deaths of civilians.

(2) The Liberty ship S.S. John Harvey was sunk with a cargo of **mustard gas**. This book brings out the cover up of this very dangerous gas cargo at the time and what has transpired since. It tells what the situation is today.

Reminick's <u>Patriots and Heroes</u> has thrilling true stories about every day life in the Merchant Marine all over the world in WWII. Gerald Reminick is a college professor with two masters degrees who gave up the sea to do research and write. All of his stories are true in this exciting book.

Sawyer and Mitchell in <u>The Liberty Ships</u> research the final destination of every Liberty. These two Englishmen are both experienced shipping men who have done a very thorough job on tracking every Liberty ship that has been constructed. This work and The <u>Liberty Ships From A to Z</u> are absolute requirements for any serious Liberty ship historian.

"Ship Losses in the Gulf of Mexico During WII" pinpoints where each ship is attacked and the ships that are sunk in the Gulf. Few Americans know the extent of our losses that are so close to home. The large number of ships sunk by German U-Boats in the U.S.A.'s own backyard is almost unbelievable The number is astounding!

"Ships of the American Merchant Marine at War" is the final report to the President of The United States by Admiral E. S. Land, Administrator of the W.S.A. (War Shipping Administration). It traces the W.S.A. from its creation on February 7, 1942, until it is dissolved on March 2, 1946. It covers the Liberty from inception to last construction. This should be mandatory reading for every high school student in The United States.

The S.S. Jeremiah O'Brien Liberty ship gives us recent information on one of the only two Liberties remaining intact. There is a cruise program for those who are desirous to actually spend time on a harbor cruise. At a certain time each year bay cruises are conducted. The trip may have a wreath casting ceremony; there may be a marriage; someone's ashes may be cast into the sea etc.etc.

The Liberty ships of WWII relates the building of the S.S. Robert E. Perry that had the distinction of setting a world's record for the fastest construction of a Liberty Ship. Photos, which are included, show scenes of actual construction. This ship that was practically "slapped" together proved to be pretty sturdy—sailing until 1963. Not bad for a ship built to last only five years!

"The Mighty Liberties" traces the start of the largest shipbuilding program in the history of the world with Henry J. Kaiser pointing to a mud flat. Henry J Kaiser dumbfounded the English delegation with his "mud flat" statement and gesture, but this man was to become the greatest shipbuilder in history. His inventive perfection of the use of welding reduced the time of ship completion, cut costs and got the ship into action much sooner. Competitors quickly copy his methods.

<u>U.S. Merchant Marine</u> Turner Publishers gives the reader not only an insight of WWII events but also gives many glimpses into the lives of WWII seamen almost a half century later. Turner covers not just the Liberty ship but also other ships, as well, along with excellent coverage of USMM history before and during WWII.

Burt Young in "Should Veteran Status Be Dependent on a Kangaroo Court" presents one of the best thoroughly documented proofs that Merchant Seamen should be given the same discharge cutoff date December 31, 1946, as all other branches of the services.

The War Shipping Administration (WSA) created by Executive Order No.9054 on February 7,1942, is the agency that created the world premier shipping organization – The United States Merchant Marine.

Some subject matter included may not be documented, but it is factual coming from men who have been there. It includes facts from two men who lost ships.

Captain Arthur R. Moore's book, A Careless Word—A Needless Sinking 8th Edition is now available (August 2006) This reference book covers all WW II ships and Z-Men losses and is a wealth of other information.

If further books on The Merchant Marine are desired, the Glencannon Press is an excellent source. There are books available on all ships—not just the Liberty.

Glenncannon Press

P.O.Box 341

Palo Alto, Ca 94302

650-323-3731

1-800-711-8985

Online Catalog www.glencannon.com

CHAPTER 3

METHODOLOGY AND APPROACH

THE UNITED STATES GOES TO WAR

The United States is now at war. In a dastardly, cowardly, sneak attack the Japanese have, while talking peace in Washington D.C., hit Pearl Harbor- our large naval base in Hawaii. On December 7, 1941-- called a "day which will live in infamy" by President Franklin D. Roosevelt-- terrific damage has been inflicted on our naval fleet and the Merchant Marine. In an emergency session the next day, December 8, 1941, the United States declares war on Japan, Germany and their allies.

The President establishes the War Shipping Administration (WSA) by Executive Order No. 9054 on February 7. 1942. This order gives the WSA control of all ocean vessels except those of the Army, Navy and Coast Guard and those controlled by the Director of the Office of Defense Transportation. This order gives the Director the authority to acquire the ships necessary for the task and to have ships constructed and fitted to enlarge The U.S. Merchant Marine Fleet to the size needed to confront the enemy. The director is to recruit, train and assign personnel to the ships where they are needed. (War Shipping Administration http://www.usmm.org/fdr/wsalaw.html)

Admiral Emory Scott Land is selected by President Roosevelt as W.S.A. Director. Admiral Land will remain Director until after the war ends and the WSA is no longer required. The WSA achieves the purpose for which it was created.

Now the country studies the methods and approach already started albeit a little late. Where is the nation at this critical time in history? The first U.S. Merchant Marine ship is actually sunk a year before the Japanese attack. A freighter named the S.S. City of Rayville hits a German mine and suffers the loss of one man. The seaman lost is a Third Engineer named Mack B. Bryan, who is the first Merchant Marine casualty. All the rest of the crew is rescued. (The United States Merchant Marine Turner Publishing Co. 1993 p.9)

SHIP BUILDING IS IN FULL PRODUCTION

The Liberty Ship is now being constructed in ever increasing numbers. The Liberty Ship is later described as the ship that saved the war. At this time, however, the Liberty is only expected to be a five year vessel. At the rate the U.S. is losing ships to the German U-boats, if the Liberty can reach her destination intact she has done her job.

There are many shortages and materials are not always available. To give just one example: Current steel shortages require the anchor chain to be shortened from 300 fathoms to 240 fathoms and finally to 210 fathoms with one anchor having 135 fathoms and the other only 75 fathoms. Even then some Liberties go out with only one anchor. Steel decks replace wooden decks so that the wood can be utilized elsewhere. All engine parts are made interchangeable; thus a small surplus one place is transferred to another. Every means to be efficient is taken and every effort is made to speed up construction.

Early in Liberty Ship production it requires a total of 245 days for construction and fitting for the ship to be ready for sea. The time is rapidly decreasing as all phases are improved. By September of 1942 in a special effort a ship is delivered in just 15 days. Later this record will be broken. The number of slips (ship construction sites) is increased to 210. Thousands of Merchant Ships are produced. Of this number 2,710 are Liberty Ships (S.S. Jeremiah O'Brien 2004 p. 15). One person, Henry J. Kaiser, becomes top man in the mass production in shipbuilding. He eventually builds almost 1/3 of all of the Liberties. Kaiser, a man of great drive and ability, is said to have the motto "The impossible is performed at once, miracles take a little longer". Knowing nothing about ships, Kaiser in only two years completes a ship in 47 days! The new technology of welding pioneered by Kaiser make fabrication possible coupled with riveting the frames and seams. Some of the ships develop cracks and some even break in half. Welding problems are found and are corrected; and ships continue to come down the skids. Liberty Ships are now put into action faster than submarines can sink them.

Before the war Kaiser had his own engineering company working on the construction of Hoover Dam, the San Francisco-Oakland Bay Bridge and other big projects. By bringing with him his own company experts and by not being hindered by old methods, and with an open mind he produces ships instead of building them. Other ship builders emulated Kaiser's newer ideas thereby improving their own techniques. A shipyard joke was that a lady came to the construction site where she was to have the honor of christening a ship. When she asked why no ship was there, she was told to start swinging it would be there by the time the champagne bottle got there.

Another individual who was very valuable to the shipbuilding industry was the late Joshua Hendy. He was a New Englander who went west to San Francisco in 1848 but instead of looking for gold he entered the mining machine business. The business continued to grow adapting and changing with the times. His company, The Iron Fireman Manufacturing Company, in WWI became devoted to producing marine steam engines. The company was ready for WWII and its first order for ship engines was for 12 Liberty Ships. This was increased to 36 then to 100 and then to almost 700. The Joshua Hendy Iron Works became the largest producer of marine reciprocating engines in the world. A fire later destroyed the plant but not before over 600 Liberty ship engines had been produced (Jaffee-Liberty Ships A-Z 2004 p.19).

The Liberty Ship shown (see Liberty Ship photo 27 b) is the S.S. Jeremiah O"Brien tied up in San Francisco, California in 1945. Clearly seen is the 3" cannon on the bow, the 20 MM machine guns with covers in the gun tubs, two life rafts and two lifeboats. Liberties carry two 18' lifeboats rated at thirteen persons,

LIBERTY SHIP JEREMIAH O'BRIEN

27b

mounted on crescent davits and two 28' lifeboats rated at fifty-two persons mounted on gravity davits (Jaffee-<u>Liberty Ships A To Z</u> 2004 p.63). The life rafts can easily be tripped by a seaman running by and are ready for use whichever way they land. Water and rations are assessable from either side. The lifeboats have to be lowered by hand. The round metal discs on the lines leading to the ship are rat guards to prevent rats from running up the line and on to the ship. The other line in the foreground is for emergencies. In the event of a fire or other catastrophe, the mooring lines can be cast off or severed and a tug boat can haul the ship away from the dock by the afore mentioned dangling line. The S.S. Jeremiah O'Brien is about to be loaded for a coastwise trip to San Pedro, California. She will then depart for the last trip she will make before being put in mothballs in Suisun Bay with other U.S.Merchant Ships. She will be the only one remaining when 33 years later she is saved as a memorial.

The Liberty Ship Type EC2 is now in full production and it is costing the American taxpayer a great price. The standard Liberty (126 vessels) is constructed by North Carolina Shipbuilding Company at an average cost of $1,543,000. The most expensive (82 vessels) is built by St. John's River Shipbuilding Company for $2,100.000. The rest of these cargo ships cost somewhere in between with the exception of 188 vessels for which no cost is available.

The Liberty Tanker (oil carriers) cost $1,858,000. The Liberty Colliers (coal carriers) run $1,892,000 (8 vessels) and $2,020,000 (36 vessels) with no available cost on 24 more. Some Liberties after they are delivered are converted to hospital ships or troop ships. Later many are converted to transport war brides and military dependents.   (Capt. Warren Leback "What Did Your Liberty Ship Cost?" S. S. Samuel Parker Newsletter April 15. 1999).

The five major accounts for export delivery by these ships that are now controlled by The War Shipping Administration are Army and Navy, the lend-lease program, civilian exports required by Allied Nations, and the program established by The State Department and the Foreign Economic Administration for shipments to Latin America and other countries (The United States Merchant Marine At War 1946 p.12). The ships were also to be used for imports for war industries strategic material and for civilian essential goods.

All shipping programs are for the task of winning the war. The W.S.A. has the job of moving all this cargo all over the world while balancing the liaison with the military, the politicians and the civilian agents. Involved is production, financing and economic coordination-- both at home and aboard. This is the biggest job of this nature of all time, and there is no model or precedent to be followed. To further complicate the problem, it must all be done during the world's biggest war in history.

Our allies, Great Britain and Russia, must receive the cargos needed to "hang on" until we are up to fighting strength. Germany has made large inroads into Russia and she has control of all of Western Europe. London and other parts of the British Isles are being bombed nightly. Many vessels (mostly Liberties) are transferred on loan to our Allies by the W.S.A. These ships are manned by foreigners; thus easing the load on American seamen.

RECRUITMENT AND TRAINING OF SEAMAN INCREASING

Now that the ships are becoming available, qualified personnel have to be trained and assigned. Recruiting offices are set up in all the large cities. Posters are placed in strategic locations saying "Uncle Sam Needs Men". Often a man signs up one day and leaves for camp the very next day. Navy recruiters who have already filled their quotas often refer young men to the United States Maritime Service office. As the war continues enough men still cannot be found. To add to the shortage, some of the men make only one trip and either do not like the sea or become too frightened to sail again. They end up joining one of the other services or are drafted. The WSA, in an effort to obtain more recruits, starts enlisting 16 year olds ("U.S. Maritime Service to Accept 16 Year Olds For Training" http:www.usmm.net/16yearold.html 2006). Men must be 17 to enlist in the other services but the age is lowered for seamen; as men are desperately needed by The U.S. Merchant Marine.

Men who are classified 4F (unfit for military duty) or 1-AL (limited service) by the Selective Service Board (Draft Board) are accepted in the Maritime Service. The Army, recognizing the urgent needs for sea-going manpower in the American Merchant Marine, release men who have had previous experiences at sea. (Army Releases Former Mariners http://www.usmm.net/armyrelease.html 2006) Some elect to return to sea but others decide to avoid the dangers of the USMM thinking they are safer in one of the other branches of the services. The final statistics prove they are correct to stay in the army, navy etc. and some never leave the States.

The three training bases must now prepare these men for sea duty. Uniforms are issued, shots are given; necessary dental work is rapidly performed; hair is cut short; bunks are assigned; etc. and a navy boot camp type program is started.

The cadre (officers and enlisted men), who are in charge of the instructions, falls into one of two categories. One group is composed of individuals who are former seamen but cannot now sail because of age or are men who have health problems. These me are highly respected. The other group is made up of men who have never been to sea but who have received a little training. In this group some are regular men and are well liked, some are just tolerated, and some are disliked and often hated. These last listed men have the title of T. S. B. (Torpedo

Scared B....) and never go ashore on pass for fear of being confronted by their students, and being cowards fear the consequences.

Training is for eight weeks but in some cases due to a crisis these men are placed on ships in just two weeks. They are told, "You can learn on the ship. Here are your papers." Trainees wear a navy blue sailor hat with their dungarees to distinguish them from the cadre until they receive their United States Maritime Service Discharge (Release from Active Duty). They also wear the navy blue hats with dress blue uniforms and white hats with the white uniforms (p. 32 c).

Training starts with learning to march in order, learning sea talk, learning a little about each department i.e. deck, engine, steward and learning <u>a whole lot about weapons, lifeboats and abandoning ship</u>. The trainees soon develop strong shoulders, arms, and legs.

The President asked congress to allow Merchant ships to arm themselves, as it is not fair for ships to have no defense when on missions for their country. This was approved in October 1941. (<u>U.S.Merchant Marine</u> Turner Publishing 1993 p10). All Liberties are to have a 5" cannon on the stern and a 3" cannon on the bow plus 8 20mm machine guns. All are to be located in gun tubs. Every seaman must be ready to assist the U.S. Navy Armed Guard as required and to take over if the navy gunners become casualties.

The heaviest training emphasis is placed on lifeboat training. Drills on lifeboat assignments, swinging the lifeboat out, lowering it evenly, duties of

USMS EMBLEM, USMS TRAINEE, USMS TRAINEES

personnel in the life boat while it is being lowered, using the sea painter, and casting off. Many hours are spent rowing, bringing in oars, etc. No one resents the time and effort spent on this training phase, for all know this training may become vital at a later date. The training will save many a life later on when the ship is torpedoed and goes down.

Abandon ship training involves climbing up and down rope ladders. This is not an easy task for men who are not used to going barefoot. Jumping into the water is a little easier. A man is taught to cross his legs while jumping. He learns the proper way to hold the life jacket when jumping so that injuries are prevented. This is extremely important, for if not done properly the life jacket can knock the man unconscious or he can possibly suffer facial injury or lose teeth. After mastering this phase of the training, burning oil is put into the water and seamen are taught how to jump into this not-too-desirable area and how to push burning oil away while making it out to clear water. Many a seaman will later survive as a result of this training. In connection with this abandon ship training, instructions are given on how to react to a shark attack. It's not clear to any trainee just how effective this action will be, but probably most individuals would react this way even without training. What are the instructions? Stay together quietly and hope the shark doesn't see you. If the shark does see you, scream, yell, splash in the water with legs and arms as much as possible and PRAY. The yelling, screaming, and splashing are to scare the shark away. Will this scare the shark? No one knows, but maybe the shark will not be hungry.

The training does have some lighter moments. The photo (p.34d) shows the million dollar casino at Avalon, Catalina Island, California. The casino is taken over for the duration of the war and is put to full use. During the day the building is used for classes. Movies and entertainment are presented at night. There are boxing matches on Friday nights. Sundays are reserved for church services. The other building shown is the St. Catherine Hotel where men who have moved into the more advanced training are housed. Catalina Island, playground of the rich and famous prior to the war, is a beautiful setting especially for teenagers away from home for the first time.

After reaching a more advanced stage of training, recruits are granted passes. For most it is wonderful opportunity to get to see large cities in New York, California and Florida. It is a chance to visit the Stage Door Canteen, the Palladium, Florida beaches, Coney Island, the Pike, a big league baseball game, The Empire State Building, Hollywood, the Walk of Fame, etc. etc. Many have the thrill of seeing and hearing in person big name bands. This is truly a time of excitement. For most trainees this is just the beginning. Many will soon be viewing things and places they probably only dreamed of seeing. There will be ports of call to exotic and exciting places, just to mention a few i.e. Singapore, Shanghai, China, Cairo, Egypt, Rock of Gibraltar, Tripoli, Libya, Buenos Aires, Argentina, Suez

ST. CATHERINE HOTEL. AVALON, CALIFORNIA
QUARTERS FOR MORE ADVANCED USMMS TRAINEES

MILLION DOLLAR CASINO. AVALON, CALIFORNIA
MULTI-PURPOSE BUILDING FOR USMS

ST. CATHERINE HOTEL AND CASINO

Canal, London, England, Antwerp, Belgium, Melbourne, Australia, Naples. Italy, and Glasgow, Scotland. For some others the future brings horror i.e. being trapped in the engine room with tons of water pouring down and no escape; being on a torpedoed ship with no chance of getting off; burning to death in oil; or trying to survive for days on a life raft or in a lifeboat hoping and praying to be saved by an Allied ship. Every trip will become an adventure—some good and some can be very bad. Church attendance is very high. Some visit a chaplain on a daily basis.

SUMMARY

THE WAR SHIPPING ADMINISTRATION IS MEETING THE TASK

Henry Kaiser and the other ship builders are meeting their responsibilities and ships are ready for action. The United States Maritime Service is doing a terrific job and the men are now prepared for one of the most important jobs in history. The United States Maritime Service is preparing the Release From Active Duty Form 16-7501-3 and the United States Coast Guard is preparing Z papers. Each recruit now is soon to become a Z-Man, a seaman with a United States Coast Guard "Merchant Seaman's Certificate of Identification" with his Z number, a United States Coast Guard Certificate of Service, a United States Coast Guard Captain of Port Card and a U.S. Mariner's Document (list of rating (s)) All these documents are placed in a large zippered wallet with a short chain that says "U.S. Merchant Marine—Papers Issued By U.S. Department of Commerce in Washington D.C." (see photos 36 e,f,g)

He is no longer a United States Maritime Service trainee. He does not have to wear a uniform, but if he does he no longer has to wear the navy blue hat. He can now wear the white one. He no longer has to salute. He is now a seaman with all the credentials and he is a member of the United States Merchant Marine. He is transferred to the port where his service is needed and he is assigned his first ship—most likely a Liberty. For him the real war is just beginning as he takes his place in the most dangerous service where a man is more likely to be killed than in any of the others services-- including The United States Marine Corps. Some of these young men will never see their homes again.

MS 5
(April 1943)

WAR SHIPPING ADMINISTRATION—TRAINING ORGANIZATION

United States Maritime Service

Release from Active Duty

This is to certify that George E WARD, 4507-05786

has been released from active duty as STEWARD'S MATE, SECOND CLASS (Grade)

on JUN - 9 1945 (Date), at San Francisco, Calif. (Place)

and placed in an inactive status in the UNITED STATES MARITIME SERVICE.

Original enrollment at St. Louis, M°. (Place) on 4/11/45 (Date)

Regular enrollment at San Francisco (Place) Calif. on JUN 1945 (Date)

Recalled for active duty at _____ (Place) on _____ (Date)

Transportation furnished from San Francisco, Calif. to San Francisco, Calif.

upon release from active duty.

George E. Ward, Jr.
(Signature of enrollee)

W. E. Julien, Lt. (j.g.),
Officer-in-Charge

U. S. GOVERNMENT PRINTING OFFICE   16—7501-G

SOCIAL SECURITY NO.   Certification of Identification 3611367

SERIAL NUMBER E 618 962   BOOK NUMBER

UNITED STATES COAST GUARD

CERTIFICATE OF SERVICE

(OTHER THAN ABLE SEAMAN OR QUALIFIED MEMBER OF THE ENGINE DEPARTMENT)

This certifies that George Ernest Ward Jr. having taken the oath required by law is hereby qualified to serve aboard American vessels of 100 tons gross and upward in the Steward Department in a rating of Messman Utilityman 3rd.

Issued by the undersigned officer in charge Marine Inspection on this JUN - 7 day of _____ 19__

(ACTG) MERCHANT MARINE INSPECTOR IN CHARGE

Port of LOS ANGELES, CALIF.

COAST GUARD CERTIFICATES, ETC.

36e

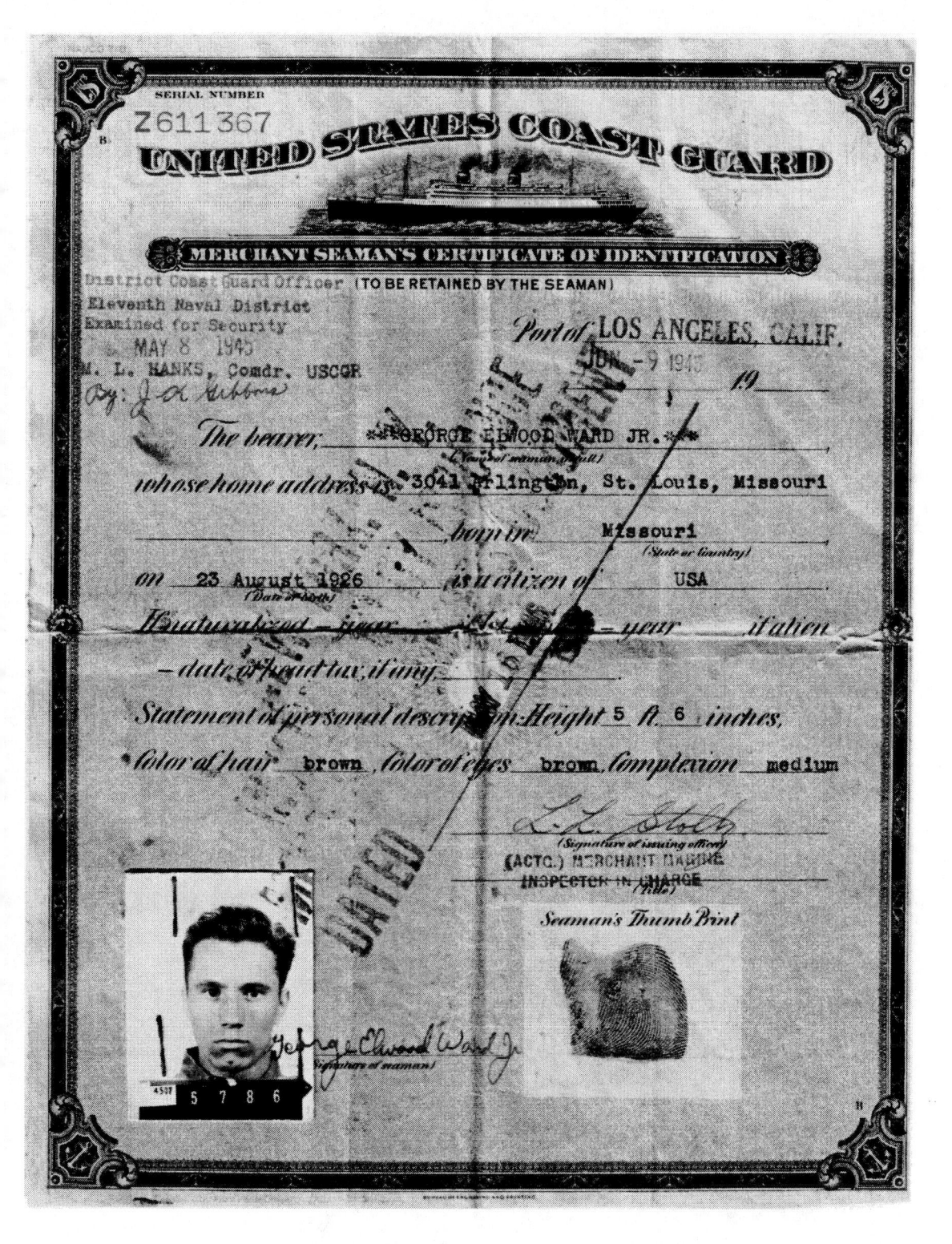

COAST GUARD CERTIFICATE OF IDENTIFICATION

Z-MAN'S WALLET

Z-MAN'S WALLET AND CARDS

36g

CHAPTER FOUR

WORLD WAR II

WAY BEHIND BUT CATCHING UP

It is early in the war and things are not progressing as well as could be desired. The U.S.A. is doing everything to further the war effort. Eighteen shipbuilders are going full speed ahead, and twenty different companies are producing engines. Ships are also being constructed for our allies. The Lend-Lease Act approved by Congress on March 27, 1941 allows for the transfer of Merchant Ships to Great Britain and other Allied countries. The list includes China, France, Belgium, Norway, The Netherlands, and The USSR.

During and following the war a total of 276 Liberty Ships are transferred to our Allies under the Lend-Lease Act. Under this act the foreign countries for war or postwar use purchase some and others are returned. For a complete list of every one of these Liberties and its final destination, see Capt. Walter W. Jaffee's The Liberty Ships A to Z. Captain Jaffee devotes 116 pages to "Foreign Government Owned Liberty Ships". Each Liberty has its name, any name changes, the builder, the date the keel is laid, the date the ship is launched, the date it was delivered and its type along with its final outcome. Also, included is a brief background of the individual for whom the Liberty is named. Captain Jaffe, in his 722-page book, describes the basic Liberty and the Liberty Tanker, the Liberty Army Tank Transport, the Liberty Boxed Aircraft Transports, the Liberty

Colliers and the Liberty Conversions. The Conversions are those Liberties converted to troop carriers, hospital service, animal transports and later are for war brides and military dependents. The military dependents are the wives and children of the servicemen who are part of the occupation. The animal transports normally carry 300 to 350 mules, but up to 1,150 can be carried along with feed and water. It takes up to eighty men and veterinarians to care for those mules. These caretakers were tagged "sea-going cowboys". These are not Z-Men.

The design, delivery and builders of the Liberties is given. Information is given on every Liberty Ship constructed. Captain Jaffee devotes 61 pages to Liberty Ships lost in WWII and 6 pages to post-war losses.

Some of these ships are transferred from the U.S. to the foreign countries while the ships are still under U.S. registry. Foreign crews are placed on them. The Merchant Ship Act of 1946 declares it illegal for foreign countries to charter U.S. ships, so the ships have to be purchased. They are a bargain at $550,000. Some are again sold to a still different foreign country. It is interesting to know that 90 Liberties are eventually sold to our current enemy Italy. The USSR takes 48 Liberties. They return 3 but never pay for the remaining 45.

The roughly 200 Liberties Great Britain receives under this program are known as SAM ships and are having this prefix added to each name. Every SAM ship is of the EC2-S-C1 type. The British can operate these ships cheaper than the U.S. can. In 1947, the British are told to buy them or to return them to the

U.S. Some are returned, some are purchased, and some are sunk. Many people believe this name is derived from the Uncle Sam connection. Logical, but not true. The British Ministry of War Transport gives these Liberties the type description of "Superstructure Aft of Midships" (U. S. Merchant Marine Turner Publisher 1993 p.208); hence this SAM tag.

Henry J. Kaiser shipyards construct the first 60 SAM ships. As mentioned before, Kaisers' yards are the pioneers in the welding technology. To further facilitate reduced construction time Kaiser now has thousands of factories located in thirty-two different states producing the thirty thousand parts required to complete a Liberty ship. These parts are stockpiled in the shipyards so that every part is available when its installation time arrives. Many distinct sections i.e. double bottoms, bow sections, complete deckhouses etc. are ready when they are needed. As the ship is being launched, the keel plating for the next Liberty's keel is already being put into place. The early requirement of 245 days for construction is reduced to a record 15 days by a special effort in September 1942. Soon the U.S.A. sees a Liberty constructed three times that fast. All ship builders are copying Kaiser's production methods and the 210 slips are working round the clock. The skill and increased speed of the men and women ship building workers is vastly decreasing production time, but it will not be until 1943 that the U.S. is able to produce ships faster than they can be sunk!

Although this is not assembly line construction, this is the next best system. Henry Ford would have been proud of this program. Later Kaiser manufactures the Kaiser-Frazier automobile. Unfortunately this auto, which is of high quality but a little pricey, does not remain on the market. All of this activity occurs after Kaiser's 60th birthday. This is quite an accomplishment for this man from Oregon who is a high school dropout.

To try to get shipbuilders to produce ships even faster a bonus system is established. Shipbuilders' fees are set at 7% but by speedy delivery this fee is increased to as high as 10%. As the ships are produced faster, the fees are reduced. The maximum profit of $140,000 is soon down to $60,000 per ship.

To attract workers to the more remote areas, the shipbuilders have to construct dwellings, restaurants, and stores. Credit is extended to these men and women shipbuilders. Some shipbuilders allow some workers time off to tend to their farms. The builders have no choice in this matter. They are desperately in need of workers. The farmers become excellent shipyard workers. High standards are maintained despite the fact that they lose some farm workers during crop seasons.

The spirit of these men and women is exemplified by the "Win the War" attitude of the workers of the J.A Jones Construction Company's Brunswick Shipyard in Brunswick, Georgia. In November of 1944 they are asked by The Maritime Commission to launch six ships in December in spite of the Christmas

Holiday. These workers go one-step further meeting the six ships target, and build a seventh ship working on Christmas Day. As it is illegal to work for nothing, 2,000 employees work through the holiday and then sign their special Christmas Day payroll over to the U.S. Treasury. Admiral Land cabled, "This is a performance unequaled by any of the six ship yards. You have made an extra contribution for the hastening the day of victory" Jaffee <u>Liberty Ships A to Z</u> 2004 p.42). This is why the U.S.A. is beginning to turn the tide. The thought of 2,000 employees working for nothing on Christmas Day is mind numbing.

Has it been tough starting this far behind and trying to catch up? Take a look at our losses in the Gulf of Mexico. Americans think of WWII as being fought in the South Pacific, the North Atlantic, Europe, North Africa, etc. but certainly not just off the coast of Texas, Louisiana, Alabama, Mississippi, or Florida. The American people are not apprised of these enemy actions and of U.S. and allied losses so close to home. We learn of these actions from a German. (Jurgen Rohwer <u>Axis Submarine Successes</u> 1939-1945) See enclosed map (41 h) for locations of ships attacks in the Gulf of Mexico. Of the 120 ships the German Submarines (U-Boats) attacked, 56 are sunk and 14 are damaged. For ship names and registry, check the roll (41i). No fewer than 24 U-Boats are operating in the Gulf waters in 1942-43 as indicated in the roll (41 i). The U.S. does not want the American people to know about this and possibly panic knowing loved ones who are in this area. Putting the losses in the paper makes for

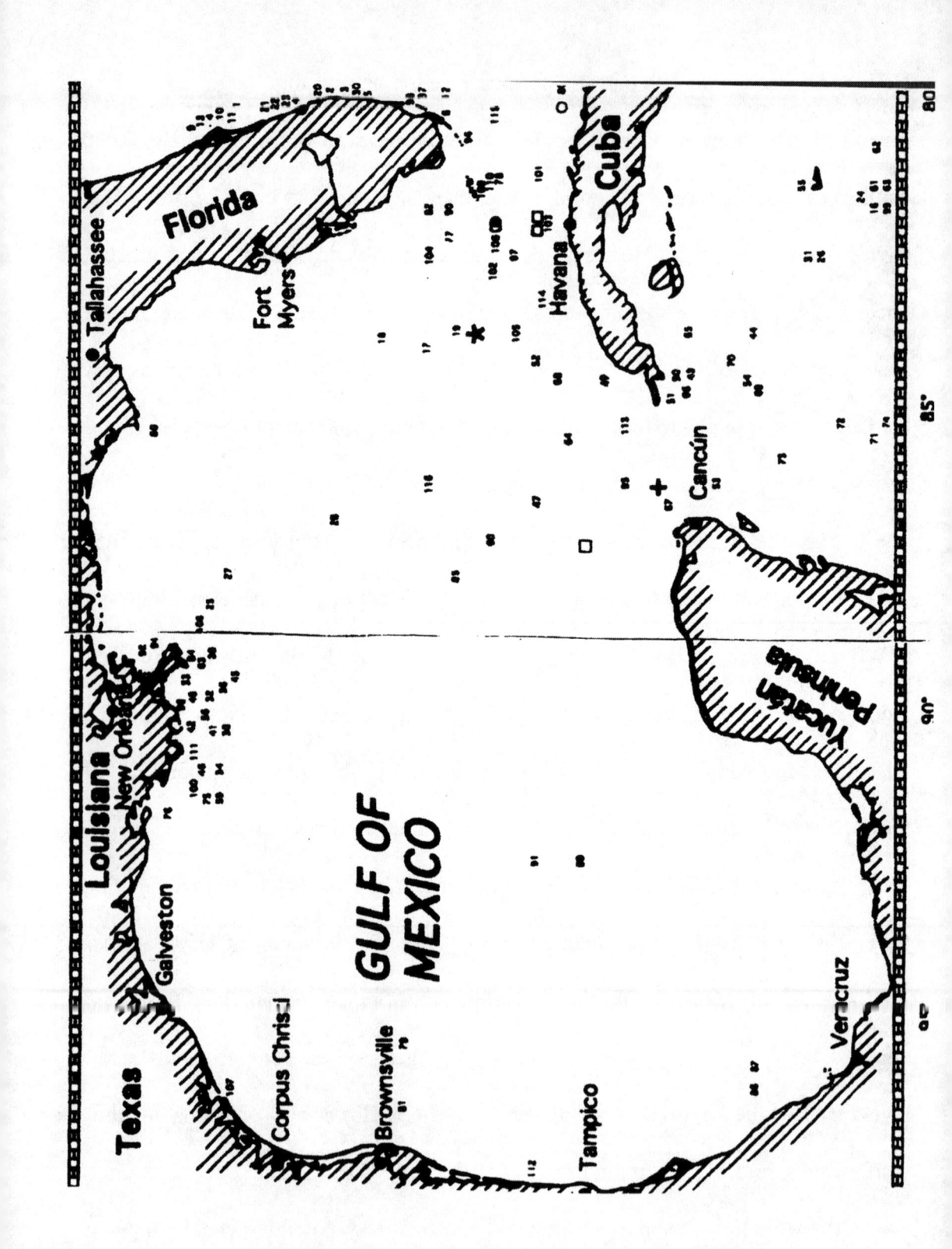

SHIP LOSSES IN THE GULF OF MEXICO

Merchant Vessels Attacked in Gulf Sea Frontier, 1942–43

NO. ON MAP 1942	ALLI-ANCE	SHIP NAME			
1	a	Pan Massachusetts	40a	a	Ninamo
2	a	Republic	41	a	Sun
3	a	Cities Service Empire	42	a	William C. McTiernahan
4	a	W. D. Anderson	43	a	Mercury Sun
5a	a	O.A. Knudsen	44	a	William J. Salman
6	a	Baurod	45	a	Gulfoil
7a	b	Daytonian	46	a	Hurteta
8	a	Abbledmian	47	a	Oqonta
9	b	Lula	48	a	Halo
10	a	Karolabo	49	a	George Calvert
11	b	La Pas	50	a	Clare
12	a	Java	51	a	Elizabeth
13a	a	Ocean Venus	52	a	Potrero del Oro
14a	b	Leston	53	a	San Pablo
15	a	Eclipse	54	a	Samuel Q. Brown
16	a	Thombour City	55	b	Hector
17	a	Manger T. Reid	56	b	Haiden Hanson
18	b	Joseph M. Cudaky	57	b	Coralealda
19	a	Norlindo	58	a	Absra
20	a	Dottie	59	a	Heinie
21	a	Joan Arrow	60	a	New Jersey
22	b	Amazonas	61	a	Allister
23	a	Heloy	62	b	Budapest
24	a	Green Island	63	a	Hampton Roads
25	b	Alcoa Puritan	64	a	Kentucky City
26	b	Empire Buffalo	65	a	Niklena
27	a	Ontario	66	b	Velma Lykes
28	a	Torny	67	a	Henri
29	a	Calgon	68	a	Suwal
30	a	Liebertyd	69	a	Castilla
31	a	Calgarolite	70	a	Tila
32	a	Aurora	71	a	Barneberg
33	a	Virginia	72	a	Marpessa
34	b	Gulfprince	73	a	Orpheus
35	b	Gulfpenn	74	a	Sheherezade
36	a	David McKelvy	75	a	Cities Service Toledo
37	b	Potrero del Llano	76	a	Gansovur (mine)
38	a	Eastern Sun	77	a	Manga Reva
39	b	Annapolis	78	a	San Jose
			79	a	Millinockets
			80	a	Medra

82	b	Bosiljka (mine)	102	a	Pennsylvania Sun
83	b	Norlind	103	b	Gertrude
84	a	Randolph Warner	104	b	Baja California
85	a	Henry Gibbons	105	b	Port Antonio
86	b	Therpa	106	b	William Cullen Bryant
87	a	La Cruque	107	b	Oaxaca
88	a	Empire Mica	108	b	Robert E. Lee
89	a	Cubore	109	b	Santiago de Cuba
90	a	Edward Lucksubecht (mine)	110	b	Mertville
91	a	Gunderson	111	b	R. M. Parker, Jr.
92	a	Unicol	112	c	Amadur
93	b	Bayard	.	.	North
94	b	Paul H. Harwood	t	c	E. P. Theriault
95	b	Thepa	.	c	Lulu
96	b	J. A. Maffitt, Jr	.	c	4 freighters
97	b	Nicholas Cuneo	.	c	1 tanker
98	a	Benjamin Brewster	1943		
99	a	Thielbek	113	b	Orianito
100	a	R. W. Gallagher	114	b	Lysefjord
101	a	Andrew Jackson	115	a	Goldsboro
			116	a	Toluluka

Note: a = U.S. registry, b = Allied registry, G = vessel sunk outside Gulf (not shown on map).

List of all U-boats that went into Gulf of Mexico and number of ships attacked or sunk:

U-103	1	U-509	0
U-508	6	U-171	3
U-507	8	U-171	3
U-506	8	U-84	5
U-106	3	U-166	2
U-504	0	U-600	0
U-753	4	U-183	1
U-67	8	U-155	2
U-129	6	U-527	0
U-134	0	U-518	0
U-154	0	U-193	1
U-158	6	24	70 ships

(56 sunk, 14 damaged)

Note: Information taken from Jürgen Rohwer, Axis Submarine Successes: 1939–1945.

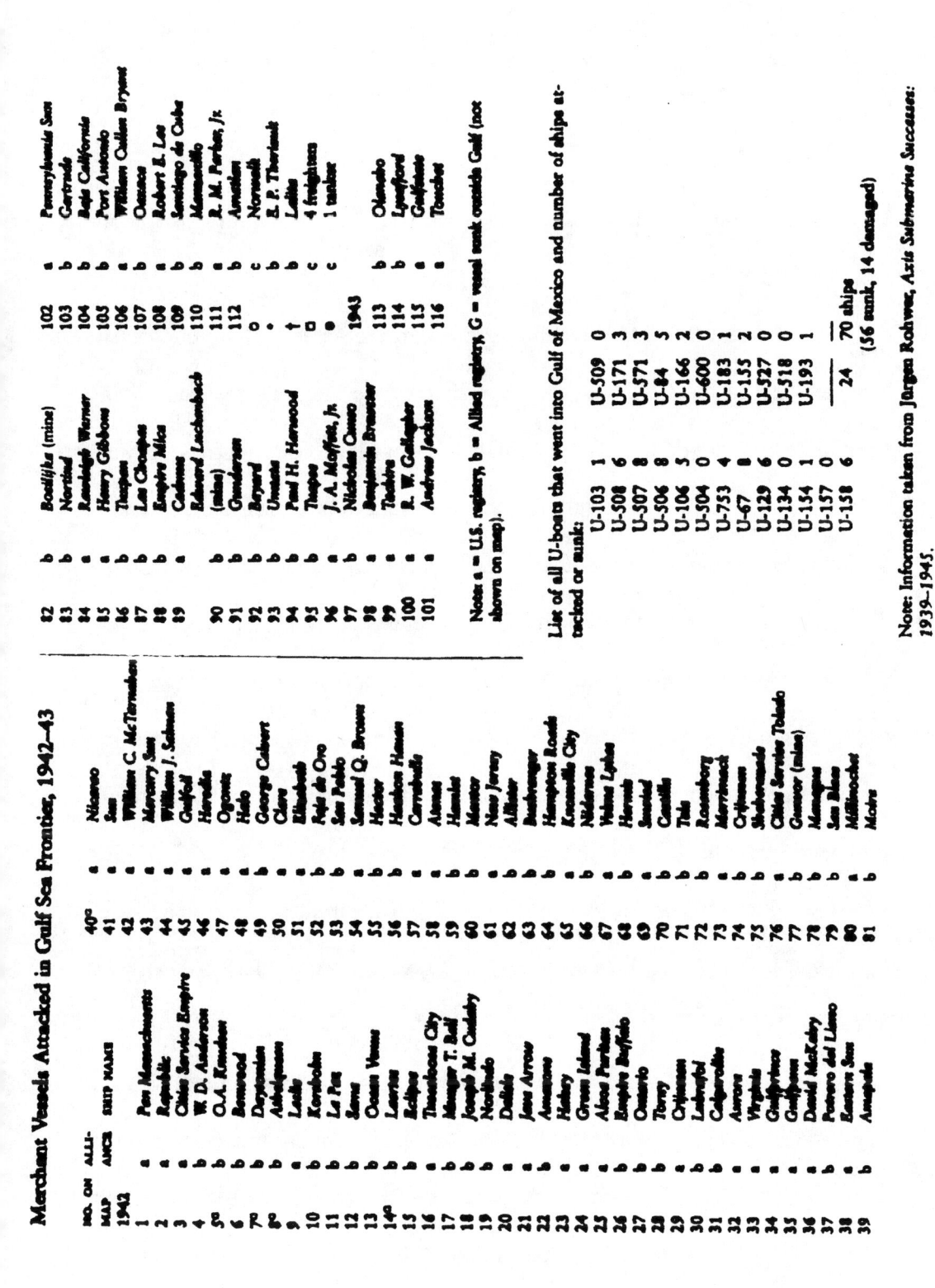

MERCHANT SHIPS ATTACHED AND LIST OF U-BOATS

good propaganda for the enemy. The Merchant Seamen know of these losses and some refused to sail in those waters necessitating a speedy search for replacements.

This is not the only troublesome area close to home. Along the Eastern Seaboard and in the Caribbean the German U-Boats are lying in wait. Many Merchant Ships still do not have guns and U.S. Navy gun crews aboard. They are "sitting ducks" with no protection and the U-Boats can pick their targets at will. To add to the danger the U.S. Atlantic coastline is lit up like a Christmas tree. At first some captains wait throughout the day seeking the safety of darkness only then to be a perfect silhouette for the waiting submarines. Admiral King requests that a "dim-out" be put into effect—not a "black-out". The second engineer of the American Freighter, S.S. Lemuel Barrows, which is sunk by the German Sub U-404, said from his lifeboat "We might as well run with our lights on. The lights were like Coney Island. It was lit up like daylight all along the beach" (U.S. Merchant Marine Turner Publisher 1993 p. 15). Twenty crewmen go down with that ship.

Yet, in spite of the efforts and sacrifices of so many, some local Miami resort owners complain to authorities. Their complaint –oil, debris, cargo and the dead mangled bodies of Merchant Seamen are washing up on their beaches. Their concern is not for the country or the men serving in the U.S. Merchant Marine but the bad press and its effect on the tourist trade (U.S. Merchant Marine Turner

Publisher 1933 p.12). Hard to believe but it appears that here is always this tiny percentage of individuals who are abhorred by the vast majority.

The west coast, while at a considerably farther distance from Japan than the east coast is from Europe, does not come through completely unscathed. Most of the enemy action in that area after the Pearl Harbor attack on December 7, 1941 is the Japanese invasion and occupation of the various Pacific Islands i.e. Philippines, Guam, Iwo Jima, Guadalcanal, Okinawa, Tarawa, etc. It takes the U.S. over three years to take these islands back from Japan, but first there is a scare right on the U.S. mainland. In February 1942 a Japanese submarine attacks the U.S.A. by firing on an oil facility at Goleta, California. Very little damage is afflicted. The attack proves to be not serious. Of greater importance is the Japanese invasion of Kiska and Attu in Alaska. The U.S. forces undergo the fiercest fighting in what will become one of its future states. In addition to the loss of lives over 2,000 amputations result because of the bitter cold—most often fingers and toes, but also feet and hands. Men in combat, under these severe weather conditions, are ordered to engage the enemy for one hour and then go back to warming stations, but this order is often ignored or forgotten; hence frostbite or worse is the result.

U.S. MARITIME SERVICE TO U.S. MERCHANT MARINE

The U.S. Maritime Service training is now complete. All U. S. Merchant Marine papers are issued and the assignments are made for the various ports where men are needed. After saying goodbye to friends not yet assigned to ships and packing sea bags, each man dons his dress uniform and is transported to the train station to board a train to take him to his first ship. Upon arriving at the assigned port each man is taken to the waiting ship. WRONG. Now comes a shock. Each man is taken to a Union Hall. What has happened? Why is he in a Union Hall? These boys who are from big cities, small towns, and farms know nothing about unions. Many are just out of high school. Following instructions they enter a large room with a number of men. Not one is wearing a U.S. Maritime uniform. Many are in every day street clothing. Some are in a variety of uniforms or partial uniforms i.e. maybe just a hat or perhaps a hat and jacket, etc.. Some of these men smile knowing that this will be a first trip for the new arrivals. Except for the older seamen they have all been in this position themselves. The new seamen think and some even say, "I thought I was going to be a seaman and here I am in a Union Hall".

Here are four men playing cards. Several men are listening to the ball game on a radio. One rumpled man is sleeping off a hangover. Two others are reading newspapers, etc.. Some are listening to music on another radio, some are engaged in conversation, and there are two men talking to their wives or girl friends. Who are these men and what are they doing? What am I supposed to do?

On the wall a large chart is displayed. In chalk is the name of a ship and in the next block is its type i.e. Liberty, C-2, Tanker, etc. The next block is for a shipping date. It is left blank. The next blank for the ship's destination is also blank, as no one knows where the ship is going-- not even the Captain. The Captain learns his destination when he opens his sealed orders after the ship is put to sea. This is another reminder that the country is at war. Then comes a whole series of blanks— one for each crew position on the ship. Only a few contain numbers perhaps A.B.--2, O.S.--1, Oiler--1, Firemen/W.T.--2, Wiper--1, Cook--1, Seward--1 and Messmen—2. The next ship listed is the same only it has different numbers for ship vacancies. The list goes on and then there is a ship with every block filled with numbers. This lets everyone know that this is either a new ship or it is a ship that has just returned and a full crew is required.

Now a voice booms out over the loud speaker. "A Liberty Ship needs a Bosun, one A.B., two Ordinary Seamen, Two Oilers, One Wiper and two Messmen". "A Liberty Ship needs a carpenter, two A.B. s, one Fireman/Water Tender and two Messmen. Gentlemen, grab you hats. We have a Pier Head Jump. Two A.B.'s are needed for a Liberty. Come on you A.B.s, help me out. Bring up your cards. This Liberty is waiting for you. Haven't you been on the beach long enough? Pier head jump for two A.B. s"

What does that mean? What is a Pier Head Jump? The simple explanation is that a ship is ready to leave right away and is short two Able Bodied Seamen. Why is it short? Perhaps the two A.B.'s, who had already signed on, have been injured or have become sick. Maybe there is an emergency at home requiring their presence. Possibly they are in jail. Maybe they are ashore getting drunk, and haven't made it back. Whatever the reason two new A.B. replacements are needed <u>right now</u>. That ship is ready to leave and if the A.B. s don't get there, their watch (duty) will have to be performed by others in addition to their regular workload. Replacement pier head jump men actually sometimes arrive just in time to throw their sea bags onto the ship and step from the pier onto the Jacob's Ladder. The gangplank is secured and the ship is starting to move out. Quite often the replacement is too late and the ship has already left the dock. Now, he needs to catch the pilot's boat. This boat goes out to pick up the pilot after he guides the ship out of a congested harbor to an open sea where the captain then takes over. If the pilot boat has already left, other transportation will have to be used to place the seaman aboard.

What did the dispatcher mean when he said, "Bring up your cards". The card system prevents favoritism and lets the right qualified man get the job assignment. When signing off a ship a seaman goes to the union hall located in the port from which he wants to sail on his next trip. He signs in and is given a shipping card with the date and the minute he signs in and the rating in which he desires to ship. After this time off and he is ready to ship out again, he goes to the union hall and checks for openings in his rating on the type of ship on which he desires to sail. If there is an open job he puts his card in and if he has the longest time without a ship, he beats out the other men who are applying. If he is not the one getting the assignment or if there are no jobs available in his rating or his desired ship type, he waits until the next call and or board entry. The war is raging and it is a short wait as seamen are in great demand. He very soon finds the ship he desires to ship on with an opening in his rating.

In short order the new seaman in the union hall goes to the dispatcher who gives him his first assignment as a Wiper, Messman or Ordinary Seaman. Now he knows his ship's name and type and where she is docked. How does he get to the dock? If he is lucky he shares a cab with someone else who is also shipping on that ship. The U S. Maritime Service is no longer taking care of his transportation. He hopes someone who attended the U.S. Maritime Service Training Camp with him is also assigned to that ship. At least, he would have someone he knows to share the start of the biggest adventure of his life.

Arrival at the ship, which will be his home for the next one or two or six or eight or even more months, is a thrill he will never forget. Going up the gangplank someone might call out, "Here come a couple of guys in 'monkey suits'." This is done in a good-natured manner, as the speaker has gone through this himself. The new seamen makes a quick mental note to get out of the "monkey suit" and get into dungarees as soon as possible. His first purchases from the slop chest (ship's store) or a nearby civilian store will be tan or khaki slacks and sport shirts. Now he doesn't feel that he sticks out like a sore thumb. He is, of course, a little apprehensive.

They do not know it now, but they soon learn that all Merchant seamen belong to a Union. They learn that there are a number of unions represented on each ship. There are:

S.I.U   Seafarers International Unions—All members of the Deck, Engine and Stewards   Departments, Bosun, Carpenter, Quarter Master, Able Body Seaman, Ordinary Seaman, Maintenance Man, Deck Engineer, Oiler, Fireman/Water Tender, Wiper, Chief Steward, Cooks, Bakers, Steward, Messman, Utility Man.

N.M.U National Maritime Union—All members of Deck, Engine and Steward Stewards   Departments, Bosun, Carpenter, Quarter Master, Able Body Seaman, Ordinary Seaman, Maintenance Man, Deck Engineer, Oiler, Fireman/Water Tender, Wiper, Chief Steward, Cooks, Bakers, Stewards, **Messmen and Utility Men.**

M.C.S. Maritime Cooks and Stewards--All- Members of the Steward Department Chief Steward, Cook, Baker, Steward, Messman, and Utility Man

S.U.P. Seaman's Union of the Pacific--- All members of the Deck Department Bosun, Able Body Seaman, Ordinary Seaman.

M.F.O.W.&W. Marine Fireman, Oiler, Fireman/ Water Tender and Wipers. Members of The Engine Department—Oilers, Firemen/ Water Tenders and Wipers.

M.E.B.A	Marine Engineer Beneficial Association ---All Engine Department Officers, Chief Engineer. First. Second and Third Assistant Engineers

M.M.P.	Master, Mates and Pilots--- All Deck Departmemt Officers—Master (Captain), Chief, Second and Third Mates and Pilots.

R.O.U	Radio Officers Union---Affiliated with the A.F.L . - All radio officers.

Going on a 441.5 foot long Liberty Ship for the first time is quite an experience. To the neophyte every thing is new and different. Wait a minute, "I'm wearing a monkey suit, but so are some of the other men." On closer inspection it is clear that these men are not seamen, but they are U.S. Navy gun crewmembers. Their uniforms are only slightly different. What comes next? First, he finds the person who is in charge of his assigned department – i.e. Boson if he is an Ordinary Seaman, Chief Steward if he is a Messman, or one of the Assistant Engineers if he is a Wiper. That person shows the new man to his focscle (room) and tells him his watch (duty hours). If his job is a Wiper, he will work 8-5. A Messman works 6-10, 11-1, and 4-6. The Ordinary Seaman will work 4 hours on and 8 hours off 8-12, 12-4 or 4-8.

All men are on duty seven days a week. Duties of seamen are clearly defined as follows:

LIBERTY SHIP DUTY

DECK DEPARTMENT

1—Captain (Master)—Command officer of Vessel

1---Chief Mate---Report to Captain

1---Second Mate---Report to Captain

1---Third Mate---Report to Captain

1---Deck Cadet (From King's Point)---Report to Chief Mate

1---Bosun---Report to Chief Mate

1---Carpenter---Report to Chief Mate

6---A.B.---Report to Watch Mate

3---O.S.---Report to Watch Mate

The ship sails 24 hours a day and the above (except the Bosun and Carpenter) work a normal eight-hour day—seven days a week. This is a four hour on and eight hour off work schedule. The Bosun and Carpenter do not stand watch and are 8-5 workers.

Repairs and deck maintenance is worked on outside the deck watch. On watch leaves no time for repairs and deck maintenance. There are many times deck department personnel will work a 10 to 12 hour day.

In port all deck department work is 8-5 except for ship security assignments for 24 hours—7 days a week.

CAPTAIN (MASTER) He has total responsibility for the ship, the officers, crew passengers, and cargo. He issues the orders and the respective individual follows them. He changes the direction of the ship to avoid hazardous enemy confrontation, bad weather or congested sea conditions. He acts as judge and jury in cases of wrongdoing and can log (withhold pay) for infraction of rules. For example, one seaman shoots and kills a porpoise, which is a violation of sea faring tradition. The Captain logs the man 12 days pay. The same man doesn't learn from this experience, and he shoots and kills an albatross. It is the same trip with the same captain. The Captain has had enough. He logs the seaman 16 days pay and he throws the rifle overboard. The trip lasts 11 months and the seaman receives 10 months pay. The Captain is not a martinet. He does not have to constantly give orders. Everyone knows his job and very little control is required. When the Captain does give an order it is followed precisely.

CHIEF MATE He is the second in command to the captain. He is in charge if the captain dies, becomes ill, is ashore, etc. He is responsible for his watch. He sees that the wheelman stays on the prescribed course. He is responsible for the ship's above deck condition and he works closely with the Bosun. He stands 4 hour watch (4 on 8 off) It is usually the 4-8 a.m. and 4-8 p.m. watch. He has two A.B.s and one O.S. on his watch and can call off duty men to work as needed.

SECOND MATE He has the responsibility for his watch. He is responsible for the ship's navigation and for maintaining the map with the ship's location daily.

At noon he shoots the sun using the sextant to determine the ship's position.. He sees that the seaman at the wheel stays on the prescribed course. He has two A.B.s and one O.S. on his watch. He stands a 4 on and 8 off watch-usually 12-4 a.m. and 12-4 p.m. In the event of ship abandonment, the Second Mate and the Third Engineer are in command of the lifeboats.

THIRD MATE He is responsible for his watch. He is responsible for seeing that the seaman on the wheel watch stays on the prescribed course. He stands 4 on and 8 off watch usually 8-12 a.m. and 8-12 p.m. He has two A.B. s and one O.S. on his watch. He is gaining experience as a mate and works closely with the Chief Mate and Second Mate.

BOSUN He works under the supervision of the Chief Mate. The Bosun is responsible for all the the above deck work which includes: chipping old paint, painting, making ready for port, making ready for sea, removing or installing hatch covers, deck repairs and maintenance, supervising watch personnel not on wheel duty or lookout, tying up and letting go, etc.. His normal workday is 8-12 and 1-5 with extra hours as required.

CARPENTER He works under the supervision of the First Mate. The carpenter is responsible for all carpentry work and the ship's maintenance and repairs in cooperation with the Bosun He closes the chain locker gap with concrete after the anchor chain is stored etc.. His normal workday is 8-12 and 1-5 with extra hours as required.

A.B. (Able Bodied Seaman) There are six A.B.s on each ship. The A.B. reports to his watch Mate. He stands wheel watch (steers the ship) (See 53 j) stands lookout, and works on deck under the Bosun's supervision. He works on docking, letting go, covering, and battening down hatch covers, working up high (See 53 j) etc. His work schedule is one of the three 4 on and 8 off watches. He is proficient in lifeboat duties and in fire fighting.

O.S. (Ordinary Seaman) There are three O.S.s on each ship—one on each watch. The O.S. reports to his watch Mate. He is learning deck seamanship under the supervision of the Bosun. The O.S. is not required to work up high, (That is the job of the A.B) but he usually does learn the job. It is the same with wheel watch duty. He is not required to steer but usually he does stand wheel watch along with the A.B.s. He and the two A.B. s each do one hour and twenty minutes deck work, one hour and twenty minutes lookout, and one hour and twenty minutes wheel watch. The O.S. works on one of the three watches four hours on and eight hours off. He is proficient in lifeboat duties and fire fighting.

DECK CADET---This man is in that phase of training required by King's Point Academy. He reports to the Chief Mate and is assigned duties as required for ship operation. Generally this sea time is in the second year of his four years at King's Point Academy. He logs sea time as well as school time. Upon graduation he is commissioned as follows: Third Mate in U.S. Maritime Service, Ensign in the Naval Reserve.

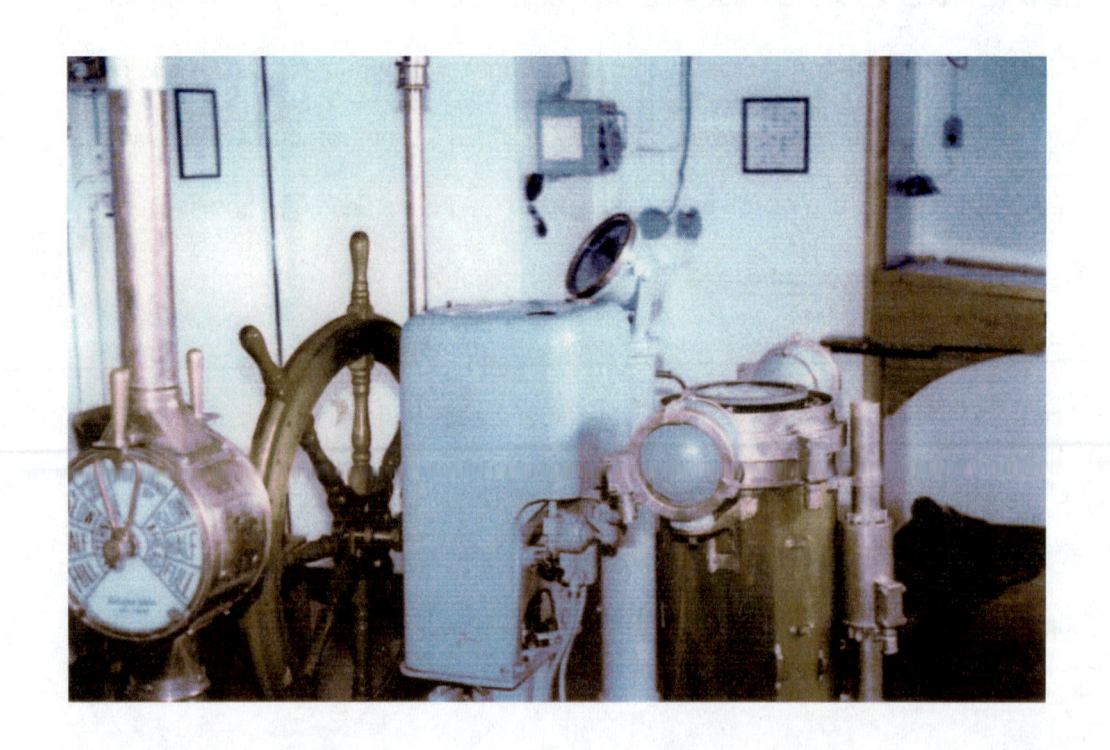

WORKING HIGH, WHEEL HOUSE

53j

All lookout duty is performed on the bow of the ship unless there are dangerously high seas or extremely bad weather. In the time of this danger the lookout duty is performed in the mid-ship wheelhouse with the mate and the seaman standing wheel duty. There is a telephone on the bow for communication with the mate up in the wheelhouse. This phone is used to report ships, lights or anything in the water.

ENGINE DEPARTMENT

1---Chief Engineer---Report to Captain

1---First Assistant Engineer---Report to Chief Engineer

!---Second Assistant Engineer---Report to Chief Engineer

1---Third Assistant Engineer---Report to Chief Engineer

1---Engineer Cadet from King's Point---Report to Chief Engineer

3---Oiler---Report to Watch Engineer

3---Fireman/Water Tender---Report to Watch Engineer

1---Wiper---Report to First Engineer

The ship sails 24 hours a day and the above (except for the Wiper) work a normal 8-hour day—7 days a week. This is a 4-hour on and 8 hours off work schedule. The Wiper does not stand watch and is an 8-5 day worker.

Repairs are worked on outside the Engineer's watch. On watch leaves no time for repairs. There are many times an Engineer and assigned men work a 10 hour day.

In port all services except propulsion are required. This floating city requires the Engine Department to maintain and provide steam and electricity.

DUTIES

CHIEF ENGINEER---He has total responsibility for all working units of the ship. He guides and directs the operation of all mechanical operations on the ship. He is the head of the Engineer Department and is responsible for the action of all Engineers. He is number two in rank. He records all data pertaining to the ship's operation—cost, efficiency, repairs and recommendations.

FIRST ASSISTANT ENGINEER---He stands and is in charge of 4-8 watch. He is the right arm of the Chief Engineer and is in charge of all day-to-day operation. His individual duty is maintaining the deep freeze. He also supervises the Oiler and Fireman/Water Tenders on his watch. He makes sure all systems are in working order when the ship is ready to sail. He warms up the engine so that it is ready for the time of departure. Warm up takes 2 hours. He makes the work schedule for the Wipers.

SECOND ASSISTANT ENGINEER ---He stands and is in charge of 12-4 watch. His individual role is that he has the responsibility for the steam operation of the ship. This includes the furnace and the boilers. He orders and stores all oil and water for the furnace and boilers. He makes daily checks for water purity. (Water purity is of the highest standards—Any impure water is diverted for drinking, cooking and showers.) He directs the operation of the watch. He supervises the work of the Oiler and Fireman/Water Tender, who stand watch with him. He works on repairs as needed.

THIRD ASSISTANT ENGINEER---He stands and is in charge of the 8-12 watch. His individual role is the responsibility for all electricity on the ship. This involves the operation and maintenance of the generators, the electrical pumps and all systems driven by electricity. He is the instructor of academics for the Engineer Cadet. He works on repairs as needed. He supervises the Oiler and Fireman/Water Tender who stand watch with him. He is responsible for the operation of the (2) power lifeboats. He runs the engines once a week. In the event of abandon ship the Second Mate and the Third Engineer are in command of the lifeboats.

ENGINEERING CADET---The Cadet serves six months sea time for his sea career. Generally this sea time is in second year of his four years at King's Point Academy. He logs sea time as well as school time. The third Assistant Engineer works with him daily. Upon graduation he is commissioned as follows: Third Assistant Engineer in U.S. Maritime Service, Ensign in U.S. Naval Reserve.

OILER--- He stands watch where assigned. He is responsible for the lubrication of the main engine and all machinery.

FIREMAN/WATER TENDER---He stands watch where he is assigned. He is responsible for proper boiler operations, the cleaning and changing of burners as required, and maintaining proper water level in the boilers.

WIPER---He is in charge of general housekeeping in the engine room. He cleans and paints as needed. (Ludwig July 6, 2006)

On the subject of the Second Assistant Engineer diverting impure water for drinking, cooking and showers an explanation is in order for all non-Engineering persons. The Engineer must see that absolutely clean water is used to safeguard the operation of the steam engine. Normal tap water contains minerals and other impurities that can clog the tubes. Therefore the Engineer's impure water is good for drinking and is probably safer than what the average American drinks every day.

DECK ENGINEER---The Deck Engineer is not found on all Liberties. If he is assigned to a Liberty he reports to the First Assistant Engineer. He is responsible for maintenance of the above deck mechanical equipment such as the booms and winches. He works 8-5 seven days a week.

STEWARD DEPARTMENT

1 ---CHIEF STEWARD---Reports to Captain

1---CHIEF COOK---Reports to Chief Steward

1---SECOND COOK AND BAKER---Reports to Chief Cook

1---UTILITY MAN---Reports to Chief Cook

3---MESSMEN---Reports to Chief Steward

1---BEDROOM STEWARD---Reports to Chief Steward

All Steward Department Personnel work 6-10 a.m., 11 a.m.-1 p.m. and 4-6 p.m.

STEWARDS DEPARTMENT

CHIEF STEWARD---He has full responsibility for menus, galley, Crew Mess Hall, Officers Mess Hall, Gunners' Mess Hall, officers state rooms and food preparation. He oversees the Cooks, Bakers, Utility Men, Messmen, and Stewards. He authorizes and supervises all work required in addition to the normal watch.

CHIEF COOK---He is responsible for the galley. He is in charge of the cooking and the galley personnel ---Second Cook, Baker, Utility Man and assigned Messmen.

SECOND COOK AND BAKER---He assists the Chief Cook. He bakes the cakes, pies, and biscuits etc. He takes over the Chief Cook's duties in an emergency.

UTILITY MAN---He does all the tasks required by the Cooks and the Baker. He can step in anywhere needed in the galley.

MESSMEN---There are usually three on a Liberty---one for the Officers' Mess Hall, one for the Crew Mess Hall and one for the Gun Crew Mess Hall. They keep the areas spotless, make fresh coffee and take care of their assigned crew members. They take food orders, relay orders to the galley and then serve the meals. They give men a second order or a little extra dessert, which is always appreciated and makes for a happier crew. The Officers' Messmen usually receive a tip from each Officer at the conclusion of the trip.

BEDROOM STEWARD ---This is a sought after Messman position. The Bedroom Steward can work somewhat at his own pace. He makes the bunks, empties waste cans and ashtrays, and keeps the staterooms spotless. The Bedroom Steward usually receives a tip from each Officer at the conclusion of the trip.

RADIO DEPARTMENT

CHIEF RADIO OPERATOR---He reports to the Captain. He is responsible for the operation of the radio. He receives radio messages, keeps the captain informed of any and all messages of importance concerning the ship. He only sends messages (breaks radio silence) on orders from the Captain.

RADIO OPERATOR---He reports to the Chief Radio Operator. He performs the same radio duties as the Chief Radio Operator.

PURSER

The Purser reports to the Captain. He has the responsibility for the ship's paper work, correspondence, pay roll, ship draws (funds received by personnel during the voyage), the administration and operation of the slop chest (ship's store). He is also the pharmacy mate. The purser is the nearest thing to an M.D. on board. If a crewmember becomes ill, the symptoms along with treatment procedures had better be in the medical book. In extreme emergencies the sick crewmember is medically evacuated which is sometimes impossible. In a few extreme cases the purser has to actually perform surgery with directions he receives over the radio.

NAVAL GUN CREW

Though not a part of the Merchant Marine crew, the Navy Gunners are an intricate part of the ship personnel. The Naval Gun Crew has one officer, usually a Navy Lieutenant, one Signalman, and two Coxswains. The other gun crewmembers are Gunner's Mate 3/c and Seaman 1/c. This rounds out a typical Naval Gun Crew of one officer and 26 enlisted sailors.

ARMY SECURITY OFFICER

The individual most often overlooked or forgotten is the Army Security Officer. He is usually an Army Captain. His duties are completely independent of all other ship activities. He patrols the ship at odd times in order to check that the Army cargo, for which he is responsible, is secure. All passageways down the five hatches are securely locked and each has a seal in place. The Army Officer checks that no seals are broken or tampered with. He checks that all deck cargo such as trucks, tanks, and sealed containers are not tampered with or have worked loose of their moorings. His assignment is complete when the cargo is unloaded and has becomes the responsibility of someone else who has signed for it.

Now that the new man is settling in, he acquaints himself with the ship. Thanks to the U.S. Maritime Service nomenclature classes he says deck instead of floor, ladder instead of stairs, head instead of toilet, etc. He is now fully aware that when he is told to report to his ship assignment that the good-bye severed all connection to the boot camp. There are no white caps to harass him, no one who requires a salute, and no lining up to eat. He isn't even told how to dress. All USMS regulations have stopped and he is now completely on his own in a town he has most likely never visited. He is prepared for that second phase of his service career- that of being a Z-Man.

The change of life style is welcomed and is for the better. He does not need a pass, but can come and go as he desires. When he is working he finds the other men friendly and cooperative. They do not have the oppressive bullying attitude that some of the white caps have. They guide him in his new position and he is now "one of the crew." If he is an Ordinary Seaman or a Wiper, he now sits (no waiting in line) and orders his meal. He has several choices of entrées' and is then served by a Messman. He tours the ship, examines the guns, goes up on the bridge, and is taken down into the engine room. He is starting to settle into his future home for the coming months. If he is in New York City or New Orleans, he finds that he can legally order a beer in a bar at age 18. In other cities some crewmember always knows where there is a bar that sells to underage servicemen. He finds a church or mission within walking distance from the ship. There are movies and other entertainment in the area of the wharf. In short, although he has not yet been to sea, he is becoming a "Z Man"

Just what is a Z Man? Listen to the words of Bob Hope's 1944 Christmas Broadcast to <u>Merchant Seamen Everywhere</u>. Bob Hope in 1944 broadcast a Christmas message to Seamen everywhere. The message, in cooperation with the U.S.S. (United Seaman's Service), is given over NBC coast-to-coast network at 11:30 A.M. on December 23, 1944. It starts with Bob Hope speaking from the NBC studio and then switches to an American Merchant ship with Hope talking to members of the crew, as the ship is about to depart. There is carol singing in the background from a boat moving from ship to ship in the harbor.

BOB HOPE'S CHRISTMAS BROADCAST TO MERCHANT SEAMEN
TO MERCHANT SEAMEN EVERYWHERE

"This is Bob Hope speaking to you from Hollywood. Three days from now we'll be celebrating Christmas here in the United States. We'll gather around Christmas trees with our children and exchange presents with those we love. Merry Christmas with stars on the Christmas tree and stars in the eyes of our kids....and stars in the windows of our homes. Blue stars for those still at home. Gold for men who'll be spending Christmas with God. And silver stars for the ones over there, like the boys I'm going to introduce to you in a moment.

They're Z-Men. Did you ever hear of Z-Men? Sounds like a gag, doesn't it? Well, it isn't. Z-Men are guys without which Generals "Ike" and Nimitz couldn't live. Five thousand seven hundred of them have died from enemy torpedoes, mines, bombs or bullets, since our zero hour at Pearl Harbor.

Z-Men are the men of the Merchant Marine. They carry a big wad of identification papers in a book called a Z book, so they call them Z-Men. They're union men too. They work for scale. Yeah, scale! Joe Squires worked for scale. He was a seaman on the S.S. Maiden Creek. He and Hal Whitney, the deck engineer, stayed aboard to handle the lines so the rest of the crew could get away before the Maiden Creek sank under waves thirty feet high. The crew was saved. They never saw Joe or Hal again. Did anyone ever make a wage scale big enough to pay for a man's life? Joe and Hal gave theirs voluntarily. So did 5,698 others. Did anyone ever devise a scale big enough to make men brave?

Listen, it takes nerve to go down to work in a hot engine room, never knowing when a torpedo might smash the hull above you and send thousands of tons of sea water in to snuff out your life. It takes courage to sail into waters of an enemy barbaric enough to tie your hands and feet and submerge you as you drown, like a rat, without a fight. It takes courage to man an ammunition ship after you heard how Nazi bombers blew up 17 shiploads of ammunition at Bari and not a man was ever found of the Crews. I was there about that time. I'll never forget it. Neither will men like Admiral King who said, "The Navy shares life and death, attack and victory with the men of the U.S. Merchant Marine." Yeah, it's Merry Christmas Monday for lot of us except the boys of the Army, Navy and Merchant Marine. Our Z-Men will be on the high seas or in ports far away from home, like a crew you're going to meet right now.

Before this program is over you'll hear their ship leaving with another cargo for the war zone with a cargo like 500,000 tons of vital supplies and the 30,000 troops the Merchant Marine delivered for MacArthur in the first three weeks on Leyte. Like the 70,000,000 tons it delivered to all the fighting fronts in 1944. Seventy million tons! Ninety percent of all the war supplies we used all over the world. These boys won't be in the United States for Christmas, so the USS—United Seamen's Service—is providing them with an early Christmas party which we're all invited to attend.

At this point Val Brown, NBC announcer, picks up the program from the flying bridge of the Liberty Ship. Gathered around him, some of the gun turrets of the Navy crews that guard these Liberty Ships, were some 42 Z-Men, members of the crew and some 26 sailors who were gunners. They were leaving an early Christmas party because, in a few minutes, they were due to leave for the war zone with a vital cargo. The USS had provided gifts and a Santa Claus. Overhead was what in sea language is call a Christmas tree—a pole 15 feet high with cross bars resembling branches. At the end of each branch was a red, green or white light used for signaling other ships at sea.

The men and their ship, commanded by a captain only 30 years old and a mate age 20, were all easterners. The captain was Roy J. Newkirk of Tincon,

Ga. The mate was Donald C. Hall of Springfield, Mass. Newkirk commanded one of the 17 TNT ships that was blown up by the Germans in Bari, Italy. Fortunately he was ashore at the time. Others interviewed by Bob Hope were Bob Dowden, Navy gunner of Indianapolis, Ind., Henry C. Bowman, Jr. Navy gunner of Jacksonville, Ark., who spent 15 days in a lifeboat; Bill Redham of Boundbreak, N.J., who identified himself only as a farmer,"Whitney" Judges of Chicago, Bo'sun, once torpedoed; Mel Wheeler of New York City, Second Cook, who announced that the Christmas dinner would consist of turkey, mashed potatoes, creamed peas, cranberry sauce, celery, hot rolls and butter, hot mince pie and coffee; Troy Strickland of Brunswick, Ga., chief engineer; and Peter Sebold of Cumberland, Md., Ordinary Seaman, previously in the Navy.

The program closed with the choristers singing " O Come All Ye Faithful" in the distance and the lowering of Santa Claus to the dock in a cargo net. The commands of Captain Newkirk were heard as the steam winches began hauling in the lines with which the ship was fastened to the dock, then the blast of the whistle as the ship began moving out, and the farewell words of Bob Hope: "Bon voyage, men of the S S. Liberty ship. Merry Christmas to you and to all Merchant Seamen, wherever this Christmas finds you! MERRY CHRISTMAS EVERYONE" (Hope, Bob "Christmas 1944 Broadcast to U.S. Merchant Marine Everywhere")

The day soon comes when the ship is loaded down to the proper plimsoll mark and maybe a little lower. All longshoremen stevedores and port personnel depart from the ship and the pilot comes aboard. Tugboats take lines fore (front) and aft (back). Mooring lines are cast off from the dock and taken aboard and the ship slowly leaves the dock pulled by the tugs. When the ship is clear of the pier, the tugs cast off the lines. The lines are taken aboard and the Liberty moves forward under its own steam. When the pilot has the ship in a safe position, he boards the pilot boat and the Liberty sails off to war.

How safe is this Liberty that was constructed in just a few weeks and is only supposed to last on the outside five years? Unknown to all but a few, over 61 (2 ¼ %) of the Liberties are to break in two while at sea—some break in three sections. This is not from enemy action, torpedoes, bombs or mines, but from the sea itself. Sometimes the ship halves can be towed to a local port and the cargo saved. Sometimes the halves float off and sink. Sometimes they are scuttled and some are salvaged for scrap. Some sink and then are refloated, stripped and then are scrapped, abandoned, or sunk. Some float off and no one knows where they sink.

The S.S. Luther Burbank will break in half in 1955 and sink—a total loss. Both halves will be later brought to the surface and towed to Japan in 1957. A new 7 foot section is added in the midships area and all three sections are attached making her 448.5 feet long.. She then proceeds to sail another fifteen years before she is scrapped in 1972. The S.S. Bert Williams breaks in half in 1948. The forward section drifts ashore, and later in 1957 is towed to Genoa, Italy, where she is attached to the stern section of the S.S. Nathaniel Bacon, which sank in 1946. As a 474.5 foot long ship she sails another 12 years before she is scrapped. Her name is changed to S.S. Boccadasse. Some Liberties just don't want to die!

Now that the Z-Man is finally on a ship, a part of a crew and about to go to sea, he learns things he never would have thought possible several months ago when he was back in high school. He learns that he is part of one of the most convoluted systems he has ever known. He is a U.S. Merchant Seaman, having completed U.S. Maritime Service Training, who is assigned to a privately owned ship, which is controlled by the W.S.A. (War Shipping Administration). He is certified by the U.S. Coast Guard and is about to depart in a convoy controlled by the U.S. Navy. Furthermore 27 of his shipmates belong to a special branch of the U.S. Navy known as the U.S. Naval Armed Guard. Should he go ashore in a foreign country occupied by the U.S. Army or U.S. Marine Corps and that area is under martial law, he is under that services' control while he is there. Also for the first time in his life he belongs to a union. Yet he is soon to learn that this crazy appearing, many faceted system works like a well-oiled machine. Each one of the parts meshes with the other parts. How can that be he wonders?

The Kings Point Academy is training and graduating bright, young officers who are complimented by new officers with crew experience who are trained in special officer schools. They are performing duties formerly done by much older and more experienced men. The U.S. Maritime Service is recruiting and training young men to man the ships that newly trained men and women are constructing in large numbers.

The W.S.A., created in 1942 as a wartime commission, is doing an excellent job under the administration of Admiral E. S. Land. The United States Merchant Marine Academy established in January 1941 at Kings Point is now on an equal basis with West Point (Army) and Annapolis (Navy). This is now the best Merchant Marine Officer Training Institution in the world.

The U.S. Navy Armed Guard is a special wartime navy unit and there is little trouble between seamen and sailors. On the contrary the gunnery training background of the seamen received in U.S. Maritime Service Camp makes them excellent assistants and backup crewmembers at the guns.

The Maritime Unions are criticized unfairly by well known columnists, Westbrook Pegler and Walter Winchell, who falsely report that the unions call strikes which disrupt the shipment of war supplies needed by the troops. This is not true. On the contrary the N.M.U. (National Maritime Union) promises that there will be no strikes and that "no union ship will leave port without a full and adequate crew" (U.S. Merchant Marine Turner Publisher 1993 p.21). All the maritime unions follow this same policy and there are no problems at all.

The shipping companies who own the ships are in the wartime mode. Prior to the war ship companies have a regular routine. For instance, The Grace Lines main routes are to the countries on the west coast (Pacific routes) of South America. The Moore McCormack lines cover the east coast (Atlantic routes) countries. The U.S. Lines have routes to Great Britain and Northern Europe. The American Export Lines go all over the world. Now in wartime these Company shipping lines go anywhere and everywhere as needed.

The seaman signs articles for the voyage for twelve months, and when the trip is over he is given a ship's discharge. This discharge includes departure and return dates, rating, etc. plus the shipping company's name. It will also include whether the trip was foreign or coastwise. Each discharge is saved as proof of the numbers of the days he shipped.

Now comes another surprise. The new seaman is now working and expecting to receive $50.00 a month. He finds out he is making not $50.00 but $87.50 per month if he is a Wiper or Messman or $82.50 if he is an Ordinary Seaman. In addition to his regular pay, he is paid extra money for duty time other than his watch. This penalty time for his rating is 85 cents per hour. After a quick look at what the more experienced man earns, he decides to acquire the needed skills and take the Coast Guard examination for a higher rating. The wartime pay fee for Liberty ship men is:

DECK DEPARTMENT		ENGINE DEPARTMENT	
Master	$450.00	Chief Engineer	$414.50
Chief Mate	$256.25	1st Asst. Engineer	$256.25
Second Mate	$212.50	2nd Asst. Engineer	$212.50
Third Mate	$193.75	3rd Asst. Engineer	$193.75
Radio Operator	$172.50	Deck Engineer	$117.50
Bosun	$112.50	Oiler	110.00
Carpenter	$112.50	Fireman/Water Tender	$110.00
Able-bodied Seaman	$100	Wiper	$87.50
Ordinary Seaman	$82.50	Engine Cadet	$86.67
Deck Cadet	$86.67		

STEWARD DEPARTMENT

Chief Steward	$147.59
Chief Cook	$132.50
2nd Cook/Baker	$117.50
Messman	$87.50
Utility Man	$87.50.

(Newsletter S.S. Samuel Parker Chapter May 14, 2001)

In addition a bonus system referred to as the 100% and 5 is in effect. It is based on the ship's location with the seaman receiving an extra thirty three and one third per cent of his basic pay, as the ship heads toward the danger zones and an extra sixty six and two thirds percent of his base pay as the ship enters dangerous waters. When the ship is in the most dangerous areas, a bonus of 100% of base pay plus $5.00 for each day in those waters is added. The young seaman, who several days ago was content to receive $50.00 per month, is dumbfounded when he sees this pay scale. In the 1940's this is big money! Working ashore for the same number of hours in an airplane factory or in a shipyard, he could earn considerably more. The seaman does not consider this; nor does he consider the safety factor. These ideas don't enter the picture. He is on a ship and pay is secondary to the thrill of going to sea.

High pay by comparison to a soldier's or sailor's pay? Very definitely. Is there really that much difference in pay? The answer is definitely a resounding "no". The explanation for this conclusion will be presented in Chapter 5.

A NEW RECORD

The Liberty ships are currently being constructed at a record pace. This ship, created as an emergency means of transporting all military men, equipment, and supplies, is built in a record 15 days. Some think there is a little jealously because of this record. Maybe there are those who think, "We can do better than that." Whatever the reason a keel is laid by the Permanente Metals Corporation at their Richmond, California shipyard on November 8, 1942. Going for a record, the shipbuilders start to build at 12:01 a.m. Everything required is on location and every shipyard builder employee works reverently to get the job done fast. Just 4 days, 15 hours and 29 minutes later the ship is launched. The builders meet and exceed the challenge of building a ship in less than 15 days. This record is set on November 12, 1942 and it is never broken. The ship is listed in the U. S. Registry as 7,176 tons and armament of 1-4"/50 and 5-21MM with a normal crew of Merchant Seamen and U. S. Naval Armed Guard. She is owned by the War Shipping Administration and is to be operated by Weyhaeuser Ship Company and sails under the Stars and Stripes. This is some record. Of course, Permanente Metals Corporation is a subsidiary of Henry J. Kaiser. This record comes as a surprise to no one.

On November 22, 1942 this ship, christened the S.S. Robert E. Peary, is loaded, has a full crew of seamen and sailors, and leaves alone (no convoy) for war. Making no contact with the enemy and traveling at 12 knots (zigzagging), she drops her cargo in New Caledonia, sails to Guadalcanal, Suva, Panama Canal, Cristobal and Cuba. Finally she returns to the U.S. arriving at Savannah, Georgia on April 3, 1943---a very successful trip.

On her next trip the Perry travels in convoy to England where an engine breaks down and a rip in the starboard side causes her number three hold to fill up with water. Repairs are made and she returns to the U.S.A. Trips follow to

Casablanca, Scotland and England. The next trip is to Nova Scotia, England and Wales where she endures nightly air attacks. Other ships are hit and some are very near her. Shells are exploding all around her—some as close as 20 yards. Machine gun shells are seen hitting the water along the side of the ship. For this action each Naval Armed Guard crewmember has meritorious entry made in his records. The S.S. Robert E. Perry makes many trips back and forth during the Normandy Invasion and on one trip strikes a submerged wreck. Repairs are made and she returns to the States ("The Liberty Ships of World War II" August 1998).

The Perry makes a number of trips—including Panama and Japan before she becomes a part of the Wilmington Reserve Fleet in December 1946 where she rests until she is removed on August 1961. In June 1963 she is scrapped, but she is never forgotten.

At about this time when the S.S. Robert E. Perry is being built and the U.S.A. shipbuilding is surpassing U-Boat sinkings, the U.S. gets a tremendous break. Admiral Donitz, Germany's top naval officer, knowing the terrible damage his U-Boats are inflicting on U.S. shipping, requests more U-Boats. Adolph Hitler steadfastly refuses to give Donitz more vessels. This stupid German decision is to result in saving countless American and Allied lives. By not complying with Donitz's request, Hitler actually aids the Allies and helps them become stronger and have greater power that will ultimately lead to victory much sooner.

Although the war situation is a little better, victory is still a long way off. The nature of the average Americans is such that they want their victory right away. Everyone is taking about when and where an invasion will take place. When it does happen, it surprises most of the people. It is not Northern Europe as most people think it would be, but it is North Africa where our troops wade ashore. Our Liberties are there, as they are in every invasion. We take on the "Desert Fox" Field Marshall Erwin Rommel. One of Germany's most intelligent generals, Rommel is a tough enemy and is not to be easily defeated. There is to be very tough fighting in North Africa. As the Americans and Allies start to win and the end is inevitable, Field Marshall Rommel is recalled to Germany.

Later because Hitler believed that General Rommel was involved in the plot to kill him, General Rommel is put in a position by Dictator Hitler so that he commits suicide. Hitler lets him know if he doesn't kill himself his family will be eliminated. There is no doubt by this time that Adolph Hitler is a mad man. Had General Rommel been alive and if Hitler had listened to him, the Northern France Invasion which is soon to come, would have been much harder for the Allies. They would have suffered many more causalities.

When the time is right the next invasion is made. The battlefield is not France, as expected, but Italy. This invasion results in the surrender of Italy. Again the Liberties are there. As the Allied troops move north toward Austria and then on to Germany, one of the biggest disasters of the war occurs.

NAVAL DISASTER AND POISON GAS

As the U.S. and Allied troops are nearing Rome on December 12, 1943 to the south a major tragedy is about to occur. The town of Bari has a population of 200,000 and is located on the Adriatic Sea in southeast Italy. With the Germans retreating to the north and Italy already having surrendered, security is lax. Over thirty ships are in Bari Harbor. Seven are Liberties. The Americans are relaxed and a baseball game is in progress with many spectators.

What the Americans and Allies do know is that a German reconnaissance plane has been taking photos of the area for over a week. The German Command decides that in order to stop the advance of the U.S. and her Allies the Bari Harbor and the ships bringing in war supplies must be destroyed. It is critical for the Germans that the food, ammunition, etc. going to enemies be stopped.

A Captain A.B. Jenks of the Harbor Defense Office is very concerned about this spying on the harbor. He states, "For three days now a German Reconnaissance plane has been over the city taking pictures. They're just waitng for the proper time to come over here and dump this place into the Adriatic". The commanding officer of the British Air Force, Air Marshall Sir Arthur Coningham, thinking the German Luftwaffe (air force) has been defeated, makes an arrogant statement. "I would regard it as a personal affront and insult if the Luftwaffe would attempt any significant action in this area" (Reminick Nightmare in Bari 2001 p10). This statement is made on the day of December 2, 1943.

There is only one 40MM Bofors gun and it is not in operation and only one British anti-aircraft squadron is in Bari. The guidance system is being repaired and is not operational.

To further complicate the Bari defense the Naval Armed Guard on the Liberties has orders not to fire on any enemy aircraft. The Navy gunners are to fire only after bombs are dropped and then only in cooperation with the tracers from the Bofors gun. This, of course, cannot happen as the gun is being repaired. The guidance system is still down.

At about 7:30 p.m. on that fateful day December 2, 1943 about 50 (some estimate 100) Luftwaffe Ju-88's bomb Bari Harbor, which is practically defenseless. This attack is second to only that of Pearl Harbor. It lasts less than 20 minutes and with no blackout as all the lights are left on to speed the unloading of the ships. The German Lufthaffe cannot miss. This attack will forever be known as "Little Pearl Harbor".

The harbor is loaded with ships trying to unload and the ships are very close together. The ships are hit in this order: first, The S.S .Joseph Wheeler, second, The S.S John L. Motley and third, The S.S. John Harvey. All three catch fire and the S.S. John L. Motley, who is carrying ammunition, explodes. The S.S. John Harvey is the next to go in a terrific explosion.

The explosion of the S. S. John Harvey is one of the worst ever and has to rank as one of the most terrible explosions in history. (This was before Hiroshima and Nagasaki.) The impact can be felt and heard 62 miles away. It also kills and wounds many civilians and destroys their homes. Flames shoot more than three thousand feet into the air. Yet, there is more to come from this one ship's disaster. The S.S. John Harvey is (was may be a better word) carrying MUSTARD GAS! This cargo of mustard gas consists of two thousand M47 A1-100 lb. bombs from the Eastern Chemical Warfare Depot and is secretly loaded in Baltimore. Not even the ship's captain, Captain Elwin F. Knowles, is told what has been loaded. This is the same deadly gas used by the Germans in WWII. Do any Americans think that the U.S. has mustard gas? What happens now?

The United States attempts to cover up the fact that the cargo of mustard gas is shipped. The British officers in charge of the port claim no knowledge of the gas. Years later Prime Minister Winston Churchill still says that there was no mustard gas. The story is broken two weeks later by the Washington Post. Secretary of War Stinson, irked by this leak, would only say "No! I will not comment on this thing" (Reminick Nightmare in Bari 2002 p 13). Copies of the S.S. John Harvey manifest are received and signed for prior to the bombing. These documents cannot be located and there is no trace of their existence.

A British Most Secret Report discloses information listing all mustard gas bombs carried on the S. S .John Harvey. The British and the Americans agree to try to keep this secret. All ships capable of sailing are ordered out of Bari Harbor the next day. Every ship that survives the attack and is leaving Bari has crews who know it is not fire that burned the victims at Bari.

This secrecy plan does not work, of course, and the Germans are quick to release news of the U.S. gassing its own troops. Axis Sally broadcasts this news daily. It would have been better to have come out and state that we have the mustard gas, but that it is never to be used unless the Axis use poison gas first. There are just too many individuals who had first hand knowledge of the gas.

The hospitals in Bari soon find that they have mustard gas patients to tend to. The hospitals are quickly filled to over flowing. The gas victims cannot get enough water to drink and complain about the heat. The victims try to remove their clothing, dressings, and bandages. They can't cool down. Many have blisters and they all complain of great pain. Almost 1,000 patients die one night and almost that many die the next night. Every bed is filled and patients now have to stay on stretchers. It is not just servicemen who are injured. It is estimated that over one thousand Bari citizens die. There is no way to determine how many Bari residents do not receive treatment for mustard gas and later will come down with mustard gas related ailments.

The only survivors of the S.S. John Harvey are the six merchant crewmembers and one U.S. Merchant Marine cadet. The reason they survive is that they are ashore at the time of the attack. They are in the right place at the right time.

The S.S. John Bascom suffers a hit by a bomb. She is damaged and is sitting next to the S.S. John L. Motley when it explodes causing the S.S. Bacom's port side to cave in. The S.S. Bascom sinks rapidly, and the ship has to be abandoned.

The S.S. Tilden is hit by a bomb which lands in the engine room and the ship bursts into flames. The surviving crewmembers abandon the burning ship. The British sink her with torpedoes because they fear she will blow up and block the entrance to the harbor,. Of the 278 soldiers, gunners, and seamen, who are on board, all but 27 are able to get off the ship.

These five Liberties—S.S. John Bascom, S.S. John Harvey, S.S. John Motley, S.S. Samuel J. Tilden, and S.S. Joseph Wheeler are the only Liberties sunk out of a total of eighteen ships, but the two other Liberties tied up in Bari, are badly damaged. The S.S. Lyman Abbott, carrying explosives, has the deck ripped open and is on fire. She has only 10 seamen who are not injured. These men sail the ship out of port, control the fire and return to port to unload the cargo. These ten complete a very difficult and dangerous job.

The S.S. John Schofield is hit by a bomb and suffers a hole in the starboard bow. Some of the ship's crew are thrown into the water. All are saved but one who is crushed to death.

The U.S. is not the only country that lost ships and men at "Little Pearl Harbor". There are four British, four Italian, three Norwegian, and two Polish

Merchant Ships sunk. All of this carnage happens in just twenty minutes. This Bari nightmare will be concluded in Chapter 5.

Bari is a terrible loss for the U.S. and its Allies; however there are still many dangerous places where the Liberty Ships are sailing. A trip in the North Atlantic in winter is an experience that no A.B or O.S. will ever forget. Traveling under blackout means exactly that. There are no running lights on the ship, no flashlights, no cigarettes, etc. Each exit to the outside has a double set of heavy drapes. The seaman steps through the first set. He carefully closes it behind him before he opens the second set. He very carefully closes that one behind him. The smallest light in the darkness of the sea can be seen for long distances, and one stupid or careless error could prove to be disastrous for a ship and its seventy plus men. Now that he is outside, it is the darkest and coldest time that he has ever experienced. He is all alone as he makes his way to the bow.

Going on lookout in the North Atlantic means putting on the warmest foul weather gear available. This means from top to bottom i.e . two pair of socks, heavy gloves , perhaps two warm hats, etc. When the seaman steps out on deck for his one hour and twenty minutes, he knows that he has an extremely important job to perform and he needs to be warm. The wind is always blowing cold. Sometimes he may catch a spray and does not want to get wet. He is at the most isolated spot on the ship right up in the stem. When he is relieved and gets back to the amidships house he has wheel duty or is on standby. He will forever remember the warmth of the hot, fresh coffee he enjoys after this very cold duty. If he has the next wheel watch, he is watching the Gyro while he steers and is keeping the ship on course. Usually he has a conversation with the mate. It is warm here and he is thawing out.

If he is on standby, he will drink coffee, talk to a gunner or seaman, wake the next watch, and perform any job his Mate may have him do. Engine and Steward Department men are, of course, inside. No one forgets that there are enemy submarines out there. He will make fresh coffee for the next watch. When he is relieved he will have eight hours off unless something comes up and he has to report for extra work.

If the trip takes him to Murmansk or Archangel, Russia, it is not the same as the North Atlantic. It is much worse. The crewmembers pray that they will not encounter the Bismark. The Bismark is the German battleship that all Seamen dread to see. The Bismark can throw cannon shells at ships from over the horizon. A ship can be hit and never see the enemy. The Bismark is eventually taken out (sunk) in what is the largest one ship target operation ever. That is another story in itself.

If the Liberty sails into the Pacific, seamen will encounter extreme heat at times instead of extreme cold. The trips are longer in the Pacific and for the most part the seas are much calmer. The ships have the same worries as any ships anywhere—the submarines, the airplanes and the mines, but a new dimension is added. KAMIKAZES! Kamikaze means "divine wind" in Japanese. This is a wonderful mission for a good Japanese pilot. The airplane is loaded with explosives and gasoline. The pilot flies this aircraft, probably a zero, into the enemy ship (that is the American ship). He comes out of the sun and aims for the midship house. He dies, of course, but that is all right with him because he has the Japanese "Rising Sun" flag folded and placed in front of his heart. The Kamikazes attacks are one of the reasons that the U.S. Merchant Marine has the greatest number of lives lost percentage-wise of all the services.

These Z-Men are now no longer the young, first time away from home recruits. They are a part of a crew and they carry their duties out responsibly. The U.S. Merchant Marine cannot find enough men, as stated before, and it becomes the only service to legally recruit 16 year olds. It is thought this might be the answer to the manpower problem. This helps but men are still needed. A number of old men come back to ship out. Some merchant crews have an age span of six decades. There are the very young men 14 years old (they lie about their ages to get into the Merchant Marine.) and men in their middle seventy's in some ship's crews. Still more men are needed. Some leave the sea after only one trip. A number have been killed or injured.

Diversity is found on ships like nowhere else The U.S. Merchant Marine is desegregated long before the other services. Because of the urgent need for Seamen, there are many foreign seamen now shipping out on U.S. ships. They are from Cuba, countries in Central and South America, Norway, Sweden, Denmark, Virgin Islands, China, Estonia, Australia, Mexico and Malta. All are working in complete harmony. Why are there foreigners on U.S. ships? There are many reasons: higher pay, better ship conditions, a means of getting American citizenship, hatred of the Germans or Japanese, and the adventure and thrill of sailing deep sea. Some are picked up in foreign countries when the regularly assigned man cannot continue the trip. In the U.S.A. a man may wait around the union hall and get a ship when no one else is available. To fill a slot somehow the man gets Z-Man papers, takes the job and there is the full crew.

Now he is visiting those far away places referred to in Chapter 3. Always there is enough time in port to do some sightseeing while the cargo is loaded/unloaded and supplies are taken on. A whole new world is opening for the seaman as he is visiting these foreign countries and they're many points of interest. In Egypt he sees the sphinx and pyramids. In Italy he sees the ruins of Pompeii, and climbs Mt. Vesuvius. In England he sees the Tower of London, Big Ben and Piccadilly Circus. In Libya he visits the graves of those courageous Marines who died there and will be forever remembered in The Marine Hymn "...To the shores of Tripoli ..". There will be an unforgettable trip to Calcutta, India to see the Burning Ghat where he watches Hindu cremation ceremonies and then he moves on to the Jain and other temples. He will see a mongoose fight a cobra for one rupee (32 cents). He is disappointed when he views the "Black

Hole of Calcutta" that he learned about in school. He finds it is sealed with only a small plaque commemorating that part of history. He may get to see the Holy Lands. He might pass the Rock of Gibraltar and go through the Suez and Panama Canals. These and other things he will see. During this time he may get to ride an elephant or a camel. He experiences many different foreign taxis and he travels in a donkey cart. He rides in a rickshaw pulled by a coolie or maybe a more modern one where the coolie has a bicycle rickshaw combo cycling instead of running.. He enjoys a swim while the ship awaits orders to go to the dock. He experiences a scare when all the swimmers are ordered out of the water immediately. They are wondering why they are given this order. They are told to look over the other side. He beholds several sharks devouring garbage, which the messman has just thrown over board. That he will definitely remember.

He learns that extra spending money is available. The first time the slop chest is opened by the Purser he is told he has x number of cartons of cigarettes coming. Not a smoker he tells the Purser he does not want any cigarettes. A wiser and more experienced seaman tells him to take all that he is entitled to. Following this advice he takes the maximum number of cartons, which cost him 50 cents each. During the trip these cartons are sold in foreign countries for $5.00 cash or they will be bartered for other items he desires. Selling cigarettes is probably illegal in most places and while the thought that "everybody does it" is not a defense, the Statue of Limitation will get him off legally in time. He becomes adept at bartering, after he learns that in most countries the first price requested is just a starting point. At first he may be a little uncomfortable, but he learns fast and soon he enjoys the game as much as the merchants do.

What is he going to barter for? It depends on the country the ship has called on. In the South Pacific he might gets a grass skirt and top for a girl friend. In Europe he picks up a Baretta or a Lugar for himself. In China he gets a sword for his brother or a silk kimono for his Mom. In India he gets a cigarette case with rubies and sapphires decorations for his Dad. In many countries he will pick up an unusual dagger or a knife. A "Rising Sun" Japanese flag is a great souvenir. Whatever he brings back will be an exotic and unusual gift.

He has become a man of the world. He has sampled scotch in Scotland, Irish whiskey in Northern Ireland and gagged on warm beer in England. In England he does like the fish and chips. He is not a wine man, but he does take a taste in France and Italy. The wine is okay but he really likes the food in these two countries. The Chinese beer is not too bad and he thinks the steak and wine in Argentina can't be beat. The steak and beef and the beer is very good in Australia but they persist in putting a sunny side up fried egg on top of the meat. This is not to his taste, as he does not care for eggs. There are places where it is not safe to partake of the local food or drink. When he is in these places he goes to the U.S.S. for an American type hamburger. The United Seamen's Service is an oasis for seamen in some countries.

UNITED SEAMEN'S SERVICE

The U.S.S. (United Seamen's Service) is the United States Merchant Marine equivalent of the U.S.O. (United Servicemen's Organization). Some U.S.O s allow merchant seamen to use their facilities and services while others do not. This depends on the local management. The U.S.S. was set up as a non-profit organization by the W.S.A. in 1942 and "became a participating agency of the National War Fund November 1, 1943" (The United States Merchant Marine At War 1946 p. 66). The U.S.S. also performs the services usually provided by the American Red Cross for the other services. At one time there are 126 facilities operated by the U.S.S. on six continents employing some 2,000 individuals. There are rest homes, clubs, hotels, and recreation centers that service 170,000 Merchant Seamen in 1944. Altogether these centers have had more than 1,600,000 visits.

These rest centers and rest homes are established for seamen who are not well but who are not sick enough to be admitted to the U.S. Marine Hospital. These are very nice centers and often a Naval Gunner will accompany a Seaman who is going in. He will wear fatigues so that he won't be identified as a Navy sailor. All but two of the rest homes are closed after the end of the war (The United States Merchant Marine at War 1946 p 66).

GALLANT SHIPS

Many American ships perform heroic deeds in WWI. Nine perform in such an outstanding manner that they are singled our for a special award. This award is known as the Gallant Ship Citation. Of the nine ships so honored there are seven Liberties. In recognition of this honor a bronze plaque is presented to each ship. Every officer and seaman who served on the ship when this award is earned is awarded the Gallant Ship Citation Ribbon. These are the Gallant Ships:

S.S. Adoniram Judson. This Liberty was in the Philippines during the invasion in October 1944. She is the first U.S. Merchant Ship to dock at Taeloban, Leyte. She provides air cover for two days for the landing area. Her guns fend off continuous air attacks while she unloads steel airfield landing mats and other cargo. She continues war service until she goes into the reserve fleet in June 1946. She is scrapped in January 1974.

S.S. Nathaniel Greene She was under continued violent air and submarine attack on a trip to North Russia. Although she suffers many crew casualties she is able to maneuver and outfight the enemy. Following these attacks, she unloads her cargo. She is badly battered, but she manages to make temporary repairs. She participates in the North African Campaign. A German submarine U-565 hits her starboard side with two torpedoes. While sinking she is again hit by an aerial torpedo from a Luftwaffe plane. The wounded and some survivors are taken aboard the British destroyer HMS Brixham and the remaining crewmembers escape in lifeboats. They are then picked up by the Brixhan. Four men are lost. The ship is towed by the Brixham to Salaumanela, Algeria—a total loss.

<u>S.S. Marcus Daly</u> At the invasion of the Philippines in October 1944, the S.S. Marcus Daly is one of the first United States Ships to dock at Tacloban, Leyte. She withstands continuous, vicious attacks by Japanese planes for six days and nights. While this battle is raging one bomber crashes on her main deck and a fire erupts. The crew is able to contain the fire. As the attack of enemy bombers and Kamikazes continue a plane crashes into a port boom and then smashes into a gun tub and two lifeboats. Two Merchant Crewmembers, one Gunner, and over 200 soldiers are killed. The ship is able to return to San Francisco. She is repaired and goes back into service. After the war she is put into the Suisun Reserve Fleet in October 1948. She is scrapped July 1968

<u>Virgina Dare</u> On a trip to North Russia she is capable of withstanding 17 days of many enemy bomb and torpedo attacks. This is accomplished by very skillful maneuvering in cooperation with excellent gunner fire. Later on March 6, 1944 while sailing in convoy in the Mediterranean she is struck by a mine or torpedo (Conflicting reports).

She does manage to reach Tunis, where some cargo is unloaded. High seas cause her to break up and her crew abandons ship. She actually breaks in two and is a total loss; however there is no loss of life. She is scrapped in 1948.

S.S. William Moultrie   Arriving at a North Russian port the Moultrie discharges vitally needed cargo. The convoy trip there has resulted in many damaged and sunken ships. Skillful maneuvering and expert gun control brings her through a series of heavy bombing and submarine attacks without loss of lives. Following the war she is in the reserve fleet from 1946 until she is scrapped in 1970.

S.S. Stephen Hopkins   On September 27, 1942 two German war ships attack the Hopkins. The Hopkins is lightly armed, but she engages the enemy with what firepower she has. With only one 1-4 inch gun she sinks the German raider Steir in the South Atlantic. As a result of this attack on her she sinks with a loss of 42 crewmembers. Fifteen survivors reach the coast of Brazil thirty-one days later.

S.S.Samuel Parker   The Parker spends six months in the Mediterranean Sea in 1943 transporting men and supplies. Throughout this period, there are many enemy attacks and she is badly battered. She is, however, able to continue to assist in the success of the North African Campaign and the Sicilian invasion. She arrives back n the U.S.A. with hundreds of holes and scars. She is the first ship to be awarded a Gallant Ship Plaque. She is placed in the reserve fleet in 1947. She is scrapped in 1968.

In addition to the above listed seven Liberty Ships that receive Gallant Ships Awards there are two other ships that have that distinction. They are the S.S. Cedar Mills and the S.S. Stanvac Calcutta. All ship personnel from these nine ships deserve the country's praise, admiration, and thanks for their courage and sacrifice.

The Gallant Ships are certainly going through rugged action and so are other ships and other seamen. Robert "Rob" Yoffie of St.Louis and his brother James "Nemo" Yoffie have both just joined the Merchant Marine. Rob is sent to the U.S. Maritime Service Training Camp at St Petersburg, Florida. He completes his training, has all his Z-papers and is assigned to his first ship—the S.S. Montana, a tanker. On June 1, 1943 off the Chesapeake Capes at dawn a Liberty Ship, the S.S. John Morgan, suddenly changes her course. The Morgan is on her maiden voyage and she is carrying ammunition. Slamming into the Montana the Morgan explodes. She sinks in just a couple of minutes. Debris is thrown over a quarter mile. Somehow half the crew manages to survive. The tanker Montana is on fire and since she is hauling high-octane gas; the order to abandon ship is given. Rob manages to find his way through an iron door to the lifeboats. Then he sees that the lifeboats are burning! He does the only thing that he can do to stay alive. He jumps thirty-five feet into the water! Later in an interview to the reporter of the St. Louis Dispatch his words were "..........and I swam like hell to get away from that ship."

Another seaman, Billy Irby from Houston, Texas, climbs through a port hole, falls into the water and swims with Rob through burning water. They both make it to clear water. There is one other crewmember who got clear. Noting that Billy is a much weaker swimmer than he is and that Billy has no life jacket, he gives his life jacket to Billy and says, "I am a stronger swimmer than you. Here, take my life jacket!" This is a noble gesture. Sadly, this courageous seaman does not make it. The Coast Guard picks up Rob and Billy. They are the only two to survive out of a 72-man crew.

Billy is a three-year veteran and Rob is a six-day veteran and they are the only two to survive this tragedy. The ironic thing is that Rob is now entitled to the Combat Bar with a star but does not qualify for the Atlantic War Zone Bar, as he hasn't put in the required thirty days or more. After a short time home both Z-Men ship out again. Rob's brother, Nemo, in the meantime, makes the Murmansk run without incident.

In May 1941 before the war starts Bob Burton is on the S.S. Robin Moor. The Moor is sailing in the South Atlantic neutral zone and is sunk by a German sub. The submarine commander stops the Moor with a show of force, gives the crew twenty minutes to abandon ship, and then sinks her with shells and torpedoes. The crewmembers who by now are in four lifeboats are given some bread by the Germans. An English ship picks them up and takes them to Cape Town after they are in the water for fifteen days (U.S. Merchant Marine Turner Publisher 1993 p.10). The S. S. Robin Moor is clearly marked with the American Flag painted on the hull.

In 1942 Burton is on the passenger ship, the S.S. Robert E. Lee, when it is sunk on July 29th in the Mississippi Delta He is knocked down by the explosion and has no knowledge about how he got into the water, but he is able to swim to a raft. He is then picked up. The engineer and the cadet working with him in the engine department do not make it.

On the Liberty Ship S.S. Samuel Jordon Kirkwood on July 5, 1943 disaster again strikes. A torpedo from the German submarine U-195 in the South Atlantic hits the ship. Again on watch in the engine room Burton, who is a fireman/water tender, cuts the fires and the Third Assistant Engineer stops the engine. While the engineer runs up the ladder, Burton in the dark climbs up the emergency ladder to the top only to have his foot caught. Unable to go farther and unable to go down he is stuck. A Navy Gunner running by sees him and grabs him by the shoulders and is able to pull him loose. His lifeboat crew, who miss him, are still waiting for him, so his life is saved. The lifeboat crew spends eleven days adrift. Burton survives three sinkings.

On the S.S.Robert E.Lee with Burton is John Marshall. At the Sicilian invasion. when a torpedo hits, John grabs a map and his life jacket and runs forward. Confronted with a big hole with steam spouting forth he was unable to pass. He runs to the stern. The door is jammed and the ship is starting to list. The only way out now is the port hole. Running he dives through and hits the water as the Lee starts down. His quick thinking saves Marshall.

A third shipmate, John Radix is on the Lee sleeping when the torpedo hits. Both of his legs are fractured yet, unbelievably, he pulls himself to the torpedo hole and then pulls himself through the jagged opening He is able to remain afloat until he is rescued. It takes several operations, but in just two months Radix is back on a ship.

Radio Operator Jay Lopez is on the S.S. Barbara on March 7, 1942 off the north coast of Haiti. She is traveling from Baltimore to San Juan, Puerto Rico carrying passengers. She is traveling in a zigzagging mode and is carrying no arms. She catches a torpedo on the port side. The deck is so badly damaged that Radio Operator Lopez can see down into the burning engine room. The ship was listing so badly that he <u>steps</u> from the ship into the ocean. He comes up with a mouthful of oil. He and 17 others spend three days on a life raft. They are picked up by a PBY flying boat.

Two and one half months later Lopez is on the maiden voyage of the Liberty Ship S.S. George Calvert. The destination is Iran. It is May 20, 1942 and two torpedoes hit the Calvert. Three gunners are killed by the impact, but all other crewmembers are able to get into three lifeboats. The U-Boat surfaces, gives the men in the lifeboats directions to Cuba and then hits the Calvert with a third torpedo, which causes the ship to fall apart.

Less than a year later Radioman Lopez is returning from the Suez on the Liberty Ship the S.S.Thomas Ruffin. On March 9, 1943 German Submarine U-510 torpedoes the Ruffin about 175 miles north of British Guiana. The explosion knocks Lopez through a door and out on to the deck. Jumping up he runs to the Captain's stateroom, grabs the codebooks and throws them into the ocean. The situation becomes worst. The order to abandon ship is given. The crew must use hand lines to get into the bobbing lifeboats, and because of the heavy seas the task is very difficult. Lopez is dangling on a line waiting to drop into the boat when he loses his grasp and falls. While falling his foot catches on a line and he is dangling again—except now he is upside down. He received a number of head blows when he repeatedly hits the side of the ship. A seaman cuts him loose and he makes it into the lifeboat. The head blows leave him disoriented and he has to be restrained to stop him from trying to crawl out of the boat. Four seamen and gunners are killed. A Corvette picks up the survivors immediately.

Less than five months later on August 21, 1943 Lopez is on the S.S. Cape Mohican when a torpedo hits her. She is traveling in convoy in the Mediterranean at night, when a nighttime alarm is given. Is it a German U-Boat that hits the Mohican? No! It is one of the convoy's own escort vessels that accidentally fires the torpedo. Half of the crew is taken off. The rest of the crew stay aboard to do emergency repairs. When the Mohican is towed to Malta, the crewmembers who were taken off rejoin their shipmates on the ship and the ship is towed to England.

Radio Operator Lopez is in a select group of only six because he was torpedoed four times. The U.S. Maritime Service authorizes these men to wear a Combat Bar with four stars—one star for each ship that is torpedoed.

Then Lopez was asked why he continued to ship out he said, "I've sat in a lifeboat and made a vow that if I ever put my feet on dry land again I'd stay there. But when I got home most of my friends were at sea, and I remember the friends who didn't come back. I guess it's a sort of personal fight with me" (Torpedoed Four Times During World War II http:www.usmm.org/lopez.html).

Try to ponder being hit by a torpedo four different times on four different ships in less than one and one half years.

The Z-Men on the S.S. Coamo are not so lucky. The passenger ship Coamo is traveling near Bermuda on December 9, 1942 when a torpedo from a German submarine slams into her. Very little is known about this tragedy, as there are no survivors and there are no other Allied ships in the area. When the U-Boat U-604 hits the S.S. Coamo, the Coamo becomes the biggest single ship loss of Merchant Seamen during WWII. A total of 133 Z-Men go down with the ship.

THE LOST CONVOY

Everyone knows of the long, cold runs to Murmansk and Archangel, Russia. Only a few remember "The Lost Convoy". Everyone has heard of the greatly feared German Battleship –The Bismarck. A movie is even made about the Allied attack and the effort that is required to sink her. An American Convoy, carrying much needed shiploads of war supplies, suffers heavy losses inflicted by the Bismark on ship convoys. Those ships who made it through are unloaded, and are then ordered to remain in port. The U.S. decides that the damages and losses are too great on these ships. The decision is made not to risk any more ships and crews. There will be no more ships departing while the Bismarck still sails. The crew wait and wait and wait. The card games, reading and Russian Radio drags on. One A.B., George Cicic, becomes restless, and he and a few friends do a little traveling. Traveling is not easy in Russia. In addition to the bitter cold and lack of transportation and accommodations for tourists, the Russian government is very suspicious of people who want to move about the country. A.B. Cicic is a U.S. citizen with his residence in California, but he was born in Yugoslavia and can speak a Slavic language. Knowing that the ships are not apt to leave very soon George and his friends make a number of trips. Carrying blankets toilet items and food they hop freight trains. They experience some difficulty trying to explain why they are moving about the country. Russians thought they might be spies. George is finally able to convince them that he and his buddies are friends and have just brought in a badly needed cargo.

A.B. Cicic is a very popular crewmember with an interesting background. He is now about forty-five years old, approximately five foot seven and weighs two hundred and twenty pounds. George is all muscle and prior to WWII he traveled with a circus as a wrestler. He challenged anyone who would get into the ring with him to a fight. Often he entertains the crew with his stories and exploits. Other times he does weird things like taking a needle and thread and sewing his fingers together. He takes a finishing nail and pushes it through the palm of his hand and on out the back of his hand. He also makes rings out of coins from the different countries where the ship docks

He teaches other crewmembers how to take a dinner knife by the blade and use the handle for pounding. The coin is held on a solid object and the handle strikes the edge while it is being constantly turned. This takes hours, but no one is going anywhere anyhow. When the coin's edge is flattened to the desired size someone from the Black (engine) Gang cuts out the center. The result is a shiny ring created by the seaman himself. George takes the casing and shells from the ammunition that has been fired to create a large paperweight. Using the cut-off end of the five-inch cannon shell for a base and a tracer shell for a holder he places a P-38 model airplane on top. The P-38 is constructed from five-inch shell casings that are flattened and cut to proper sizes. This is a real conversation piece. A.B. Cicic is a very well- liked crewmember.

As the weeks stretch into months no word is received in the U.S.A. about the convoy. Parents, wives and girl friends are worried sick about the various ship crewmembers. No mail or other correspondence is exchanged. One crewmember becomes seriously ill and must be flown to the U.S.A. for the necessary medical treatment. This seaman promises to contact each crewmember's loved ones. He follows through and all seventy crewmembers families are greatly relieved to get the news that the seamen and sailors are safe. A second crewmember also becomes ill and the same action takes place. These are the only messages the families receive for a full year, as no mail can be sent out of the U.S.S.R.

The crew on A.B. Cicic's ship vote unanimously (seamen and sailors) to try to sail back home. The W.S.A. informs them they are not going to leave while the Bismark is still a threat. Finally a strong determined effort to sink the Bismark is made involving both sea and air strength. The mighty Bismark, thought by the Germans to be unsinkable, goes to the bottom. A much-relieved "Lost Convoy" sails home.

There are always enterprising individuals who employ strength and wisdom to profit from a situation. One crewmember whose name will not be disclosed is certainly in that category. After working his day port watch he works a full shift as a longshoreman. There is always a need for men to load and unload the ships. The labor shortage is a result of men of draft age serving in the military. This young man quietly takes this extra money that he earns and purchases whiskey. Smuggling is a harsh word, so this is called American Enterprise. He quietly brings this beverage aboard ship and places it in a very secret out of the way place and soon has quite a cache. No one knows about this whiskey, or it would rapidly "disappear".

The ship is loaded and sails into the South Pacific. This young man is patient. He waits until the ship finally arrives in an isolated area where his product is in great demand. He then unloads it at the greatly inflated price of $85.00 to $100.00 per bottle. Having paid $4.04 for a fifth of Four Roses this results in a very good profit for this young man who neither smokes nor drinks. The men who purchase this should not be pitied too much; because the cash used for the purchase was actually won in a poker game or by shooting craps.

Arriving back in the U.S. this young man who seized this opportunity for gain is going to spend his profit wisely. He pays off the farm that he and his young wife had purchased just before he went off to war. He has enough left over to buy a new pickup truck when they are again available. During the war the production of cars and trucks is stopped. This is one young man who really benefited financially from the war.

JAPANESE ATROCITIES ---AMERICANS BEHEADED

Randall Bishop of Laguna Beach said, "These were indeed dangerous years for the Merchant Marines". Bishop, an A.B., found an account in a Honolulu newspaper that he sent to his hometown newspaper editor. The excerpt from Lord James Blears read, "From December 13, 1943 to the end of the war with Japan, all Japanese submarine commanders receive orders from Vice Admiral Salouju and Vice Admiral Hisao Ichioka, Commander of Sub-RON 8, to sink all enemy ships, and to take alive (if possible) the Captain and several other survivors aboard their ships for interrogation, then kill them and all the remaining survivors from the sunken ship.

This is what the majority of the Japanese ships do with samurai swords, pistols, sledgehammers, machine guns, and bayonets. Between December 13, 1943 and October 1944 in the Indian Ocean alone, Japanese U-Boats attack, sink and massacre the crews of eight Allied ships including the S.S.Tjisalak, which is sunk on March 26, 1944 by the Japanese submarine the 1-8 commanded by Tatsuniki Aritizumi.

Lord James Blears wrote the following. "British, Dutch, Indonesian, Australians, and an American (female) Red Cross nurse—103 people total received the above treatment. All were murdered in cold blood. Three Dutch officers, one British Indian seaman, and myself, Second

Radio Officer J.R. Blears (British) lived. How we survived the swords and machine guns and being left for dead 1,200 miles from land is another story.

I (Lord James Blears) feel that these facts should be noted in memory of my shipmates and hundreds of others who were murdered and who are not around to write about it."

"Peace on earth to all" (U.S. Merchant Marine Turner Publisher 1993 p.42-43)

On July 2, 1944 one of the most inhumane acts of WWII occurs. The S.S.Jean Nicolet is traveling through the Indian Ocean with a general cargo. In addition to her normal crew of 42 seamen and 28 navy gunners, she has on board thirty passengers and one U.S. Army medic. It is night when the Nicolet is hit by two torpedoes. The Japanese submarine surfaces and proceeds to shell her. In spite of this action everyone aboard somehow manages to abandon ship in four lifeboats and on two rafts.

The horror becomes worse. The crew are now Japanese prisoners on the deck of the submarine. Their hands are tied together with wire behind their backs. Some are made to run a gantlet between two lines of Japanese Seamen. The prisoners are struck by clubs and knives as they run. Then one big Japanese bayonets them and they are tossed into the ocean. Others are being battered, clubbed, knifed and bayoneted. Suddenly a plane, thought to be British, approaches and the submarine dives with those Americans still alive on deck.

After freeing themselves from their wire binding, they continue to tread water and assist others with their wire binding. The H.M.I.S. Hoxa picks them up. Out of the one hundred total crew and passengers only 23 survive. The S. S. Jean Nicolet's Captain, who has been placed on the submarine, is never heard of again. The victims include 30 Z-Men, 19 gunners, the Army medic, and 27 passengers. A number of these victims are beheaded in front of their fellow Americans, who know that their time is next. Thank God for that airplane. As Captain Moore states at King's Point Academy at a Liberty Shipman Reunion in the 1990's –"Had it not been for that airplane the world would never have known of this atrocity". Where are these Japanese sailors today? Most undoubtedly dead, but some may still be alive. Do their consciences bother them?

The Japanese Submarine Commander commits hara-kari (suicide) in August 1945 when his later command, the large submarine 1-400, is taken over by the U.S. Navy (The Liberty Ships-Sawyer and Mitchell, 1985 p. 129).

It would appear that the Japanese have never heard of the Geneva Convention. A number of Americans could have survived if the Japanese submarine crew had followed the rules.

SHIPBOARD PROBLEMS

Captain Frank F. Farrar starts sailing as a deck boy when he is just sixteen years old. The U.S.A. is in the grip of the Great Depression and the American Merchant Marine is third rate. Captain Farrar sees this sorry shipping industry rise up to become the largest Merchant Marine in history. During this period Captain Farrar learns his trade working up the ladder to Captain. In <u>A Ship's Log Book</u>, he relates some of the human problems associated with being a seaman. He has a "pier head jump" on a Liberty Ship in Baltimore. When he arrives at the dock and takes a look at the ship, he sees that it doesn't seem quite right. It appears to be resting on the bottom. He wonders if she has a leak. Borrowing the Naval Gunnery Officer's waterproof flashlight he sticks the light under the water to check the Plimsoll mark. He knows that the Liberty is going into the North Atlantic and she should be loaded only to WNA (Winter North Atlantic). He finds the Plimsoll mark two feet below the water level. This means that the ship is way overloaded. As he is the Chief Mate it is his duty to check this out. He goes down to the Coast Guard Headquarters and is pushed from officer to officer. By this time he is really steaming. About to blow his top Chief Farrar is finally sent to the right man, a Lieutenant who will talk to him. This young officer looking down on this Chief Mate tells him, "Now then, Mr. Mate. Maybe you've overlooked the obvious fact that there is a great war raging out there. In wartime we always take calculated risks...and some that aren't calculated" (<u>A Ship's Log Book Farrar</u> 1988 – p. 191).

    This is when Chief Mate Farrar blows up, calling the Lieutenant "a little pipsqueak" and letting him know he was sailing the ships when the Lieutenant was still in grammar school. He proceeds to tell this young Coast Guard Officer what he thinks of his regulations. He calls the Lieutenant "Junior" and says that he will still be sitting at his nice safe desk on his skinny backside telling some one else there's a war on while seventy-two men will be on a dangerously overloaded ship in the North Atlantic. The Lieutenant then sends him to the Commander who promises to send out an inspection team. The Chief asks when he can expect the team and he is told that he can expect the team at 8 a.m. the next morning.

When he arrives back at the ship Chief Mate Farrar checks the loading manifest and immediately finds the reason for the overload. The holds contain iron, steel, railroad rails, rail spikes, rail car wheels, and axles. When he is about half way through his dinner a tugboat arrives and the Liberty is moved to another dock. This has not been a great day, but the next day proves to be even worse.

Though the ship is already overloaded, the longshoremen start to load four locomotives and four tenders as deck cargo. The inspection team never arrives and the Coast Guard Commander is called. This office informs Farrar that the Commander is out in the field and won't be back until next week. Oh, yes, the Lieutenant is with him. The Chief Mate complains to the ship's captain but he gets no satisfaction. He is told that the ship will sail as soon as the locomotives are chained down. The next order further infuriates Chief Mate Farrar. He is told that his deck gang is to lubricate the deck cargo daily.

The heavily overloaded Liberty is bound for France. The second day the ship is hit by winter seas, and the box holding the lubricants washes overboard. A couple of days later the port bulwark cracks open. The ship is made ready to execute abandonment, if necessary, and is forced to drop out of the convoy. The Liberty travels at half speed but does get back to Halifax. A decision is made to unload the locomotives. Two are removed and ship repairs are made. Now, to Chief Mate Farrar's horror, the other two locomotives and tenders are not removed and the two locomotives that had been unloaded are put back on the ship!

The Liberty sets sail again and makes it past Gibraltar to unload at Marseilles. When the ship gets back to the States, Chief Mate Farrar is paid off. All crewmembers are paid off at the end of each voyage. The next trip for the Liberty is to Murmansk with a different Chief Mate. On this trip she is torpedoed and she sinks.

Although the Plimsoll episode does not end in tragedy, it very well could have. Many ships in WWII violate the Plimsoll mark levels that in peacetime would have the insurance companies screaming. To violate the Plimsoll mark would have cost someone his job. When lives and cargo are at stake, there should be no uncalculated risks and calculated risks should be well calculated.

Captain Farrar, sailing on another ship as Chief Mate, has a different problem. While the ship is unloading cargo at Boue in Northern Africa, Chief Mate Farrar is making his rounds checking the cargo handling gear. As he looks down hatch number three he finds the longshoreman's crew from England is roaring drunk. The cargo is ale and cases of it are scattered all over the area. As he is going down in number 3 hatch he confronts two drunken workers from hatch number 1. They are taking cases of the ale. The men become belligerent and the Chief Mate is unable to reason with them. He beats a fast retreat up the ladder.

The problem intensifies because the winch operator closes the door to the hatch and dogs (locks) it and it is firmly shut. Farrar bangs on the door and yells, the only response that he gets is cursing. He climbs up to the ventilator and looking like an animal in a cage, he shouts until the Captain sees him. Enraged that his Chief Mate is locked up, he yells, "Well damn my soul, no Limey's going to lock up my chief officer. I'll be right down there" (A Ship's Log Book Farrar 1988 p.155). The Chief Mate implores the Captain, who only weighs about 130 pounds, "not to mess around with the big ape". The Captain does not listen. He starts screaming as he jumps on the longshoreman's back. Both fall to the deck and the Battalion Captain walks up. His comment is, "Ere, 'ere, chaps. What the 'ell is going on 'ere? Canadian ale, is it? Almost as good as spirits." He then picks up a bottle and proceeds to drink.

The Chief Mate is released. He tries to get the Army Captain to stop the stealing but to no avail, and the ale is cleaned out. The Chief Mate, rationalizing, decides that if the British Longshoremen want to steal from their own buddies—let them. The ale is headed for the NAAFI, the British PX (ship's store). There is absolutely no way that he can stop them anyhow.

Seaman John Brady signed on the S.S. Beaconhill —a ship destined to have crew problems. Even though the crewmembers never know the ship's destination when they sign on, sometimes it becomes pretty clear where they are going by the gear that is issued. When the ship provides the seamen with felt boots, a sheepskin coat, a fur lined hat and a rubber suit with a light on it they know that they are going to Russia.

The Beaconhill, loaded with high-octane gas, leaves New York in convoy. German Luftwaffe planes, out of Norway, attack the convoy off North Cape for two days. The convoy is split with half (fifteen ships) going to Murmansk and the other fifteen ships, including the S.S. Beaconhill, going to Molotovsk. As they enter the White Sea, a big well-armed Russian Ice Breaker takes over the lead. The German planes again attack. The bombs miss, but they drop incendiaries that land on the deck and start fires. The crew puts out the fires. A Russian escort joins the convoy and the German planes are forced to return to Norway.

The Beaconhill arrives at Molotovsk on March second and the gas is unloaded and the ship is sent to Archangel. She will now take the place of the Norwegian tanker S.S. Marathon that has been severely damaged. The American ship makes sixteen trips in these frigid waters in the next six months. The food supplies are getting low and there is the constant strain of danger.

The crew problems begin. The cook goes to the Chief Steward and wants to know how he is expected to feed the crew with the food shortage. They argue and the Chief Steward, who is of Scandinavian descent, knocks the cook down breaking his leg. The cook, being English, is taken aboard a British Corvette for treatment. Fights among the crew follow this incident. One seaman must be removed from the ship when he tries to stab a shipmate. Removing him is not easy. He takes an axe and locks himself in his focscle. The Marine Sergeant tells him if he doesn't come out, they will come in and get him, and that he could possibly be killed. He lays down the axe and gives up. He is taken off the ship in handcuffs.

Fights continue and the six months stretches into nine months. One of the crew takes his trombone to the Intourist (hotel) intending to sit in with the local Russian band. As he starts to play a Russian officer tells him "Nyet dobriy". (Don't play it) The musician and his brother, who is a crewmember, get into a fight with the Russian officer. The trombonist strikes the officer and both seamen land in prison. They are released prior to the ship's next run to Murmansk. This is not to be the end of this incident.

The S.S. Beaconhill is ready to sail for England in a convoy. At the last minute a small boat comes out and removes the trombone player. He is put in a prison camp for six months doing hard labor for fourteen hours a day and was given very little food.

The American Embassy in Scotland claims nothing can be done for the seaman because the ship is flying a Panamanian flag and not an American flag.

The ship has an all American gun crew and mostly American Merchant crew. The ship arrives back in the U.S.A. at Christmas time in 1944. So much for our ally friend (?) Russia. (<u>Patriots and Heroes</u> Reminick 2000 p.97)

The old timers tell the young seamen that should the seamen get into trouble, they will quite often find the U.S. Embassy very unsympathetic and that it will render little or no assistance. If trouble arises the seamen are advised to go to the British Embassy. With a long seafaring history the British are more apt to help the seamen (even if they are not British) if the reason for incarceration is not really serious. The best course is to follow the local laws and not get into trouble.

Not all the problems are caused by the enemy. Crossing the equator is a bit of a problem (maybe harassment is a better word) for those men passing that line for the first time. The shellbacks are those who have crossed the equator before. How rough it is for the pollywogs (first time crossers) depends on the shellbacks' imagination and creativity.

Neptunus Rex comes out of the ocean (from the bow area) and the shellbacks greet him with bows and shouts. He comes aboard to see that all polly-wogs are "gathered to our fold and are duly initiated into the "SOLEMN MYSTERIES OF THE ANCIENT ORDER OF THE DEEP". Davy Jones, his Majesty's scribe, is there to assist.

Now the fun begins. The pollywogs, who are blindfolded and wearing only shorts, are given something to drink. Hope they like hot sauce. There is the paddling line. They must kiss the Royal Queen's foot. The queen is usually a fat seaman with a mop bottom for a wig and who is wearing a crazy robe and has one shoe off. The pollywog actually kisses someone's hand. When the blindfold is removed, he is facing the Queen's foot. The Royal Barber gives each pollywog a haircut and then applies hair lotion. The haircut consists of two or three big cuts to the scalp followed by a "lotion of graphite and dirty oil". After the ceremony most of the pollywogs shave their heads as soon as they can. They know that the hair will grow back before the voyage is over.

On one ship an Assistant Radio Operator breaks loose from the shellbacks and runs to his room cursing everyone. The Chief Mate tells him he should "take it like a man just like everyone else, or he will be sorry. The retort is "Go to hell".

With the Equator Crossing over shipboard life resumes. The night before the ship is to make its final docking—it happens. A number of crewmembers rush into the Assistant Radio Operator's room and the Equator ceremony is completed. He receives his haircut (just a little more than the others received), and he gets the graphite and oil treatment. When the Liberty Ship docks the next day, the radio operator departs as soon as shore leave is posted. He takes his bags and does not return to the ship.

Many problems are encountered during a war. Sometimes the problem involves a convoy, an individual ship, a crew, or an individual (s). A new Liberty Ship, the Raymond V. Ingersoll, on its first convoy is sailing for Italy in

November 1944. A serious storm causes the loss of an A.B. washed overboard. Two other Z-Men on different ships in that convoy are also swept to their deaths. A Second Cook on the S.S. Olney has appendicitis that requires his being transferred to another ship. In heavy seas a destroyer shoots the Olney a life buoy. While being transferred in heavy seas to the destroyer, the cook dips into the ocean several times.

The S.S.Stephen Hopkins in April of 1942 is on her maiden voyage. Scheduled to go around the world she stops in New Zealand and Australia. Encountering a typhoon she is slowed down, but she does drop her load of grain in South Africa and picks up a load of bauxite. From there she heads out into the South Atlantic. Early on the morning of Sunday September 27, 1942 her problems begin. The Hilfskreuzer Stier and her supply ship Tannenfels, both heavily armed raiders, start shelling the Hopkins. The Hopkins fights back against the Stier, which is cruiser size and strength. Both ships go down with only 21 Hopkins crewmembers who make it to the lifeboats.

German ships usually rescue crews from the ships that they sink, but the Tannenfels picked up only the Stier survivors and left. The Americans use their compass to set sail for South America 1600 miles away. The problem is food. They ration the food, but they give triple rations to the injured, six of whom eventually die. Even with their great hunger all fifteen have a strange compassion for a large bird who lands in the boat with them. The bird is caught in the storm and is exhausted. They catch the bird and think, "Here is a meal." They realize that the bird is fighting for its life as they are. They cannot hurt it. After allowing the bird to regain its strength for two days, they let it fly off.

When they are out of water, they pray for rain and it comes. After being adrift for 31 days, they sight land. They reach the coast of Brazil and are met by natives who assist them. They are taken to a small village by dugout canoes. Of the 15 survivors all return to sea, but sadly only 3 survive the war (Maritime American Merchant Veterans 2006 p.91-93).

This is the S.S. Stephen Hopkins listed as a Gallant Ship earlier. The S.S. Stephen Hopkins is the only Merchant Ship to sink an enemy Man of War in WWII.

There is a German U-Boat Captain who operates off the west coast of Africa. He sinks a number of Allied ships, but always surfaces and picks up survivors. The German Captain is a kind individual who is just doing his job. The Captain who has dark red hair always chats with prisoners. He speaks good English. If there is no way to transfer survivors to a German Stalag (Prison Camp), he puts them ashore on the west coast of Africa. No one knows his name or if he survives the war. If a sub sinks an Allied Ship, the crew is thankful if this red headed German U-Boat Commander surfaces rather than a Japanese Captain.

Men who abandon ships are confronted with many dangers—burning oil, being dragged down with the ship, being machine gunned by the enemy, being tangled in lines, not having a life jacket, etc.

The U.S. Coast Guard provides the best life jacket available. The seaman now has a life jacket that is much softer than the type that he trained with in the U.S. Maritime Service. There is far less chance of the life jacket striking the seaman in the face or head and rendering him unconscious when he hits the water. Attached to the life jacket is a Coast Guard whistle and knife. The whistle is invaluable in heavy smoke or fog, and at night it is an aid in finding others. The knife gives a seaman a chance to cut himself free from binding lines if necessary. The knife is designed so a man can open it with one hand should the other hand be caught or is not free. The knife (See knife p 113 k) has a blade extending from the handle. The seaman grips the blade with one hand and opens the knife by rubbing the extending end of the handle on his leg or some other object. A small chain to the lifejacket connects both the knife and whistle. This prevents them from being lost if they slip out of the seaman's hand.

It is the fervent prayer of seamen not to be torpedoed, not to be bombed, and not to be hit by a mine. Extra care is taken at all times to lower the risk of an attack. A press release from Washington on June 14, 1942 warns what can happen if someone is negligent. A German submarine Captain broadcasts through Radio Stuttgart that his U-Boat has sunk a freighter. While the submarine

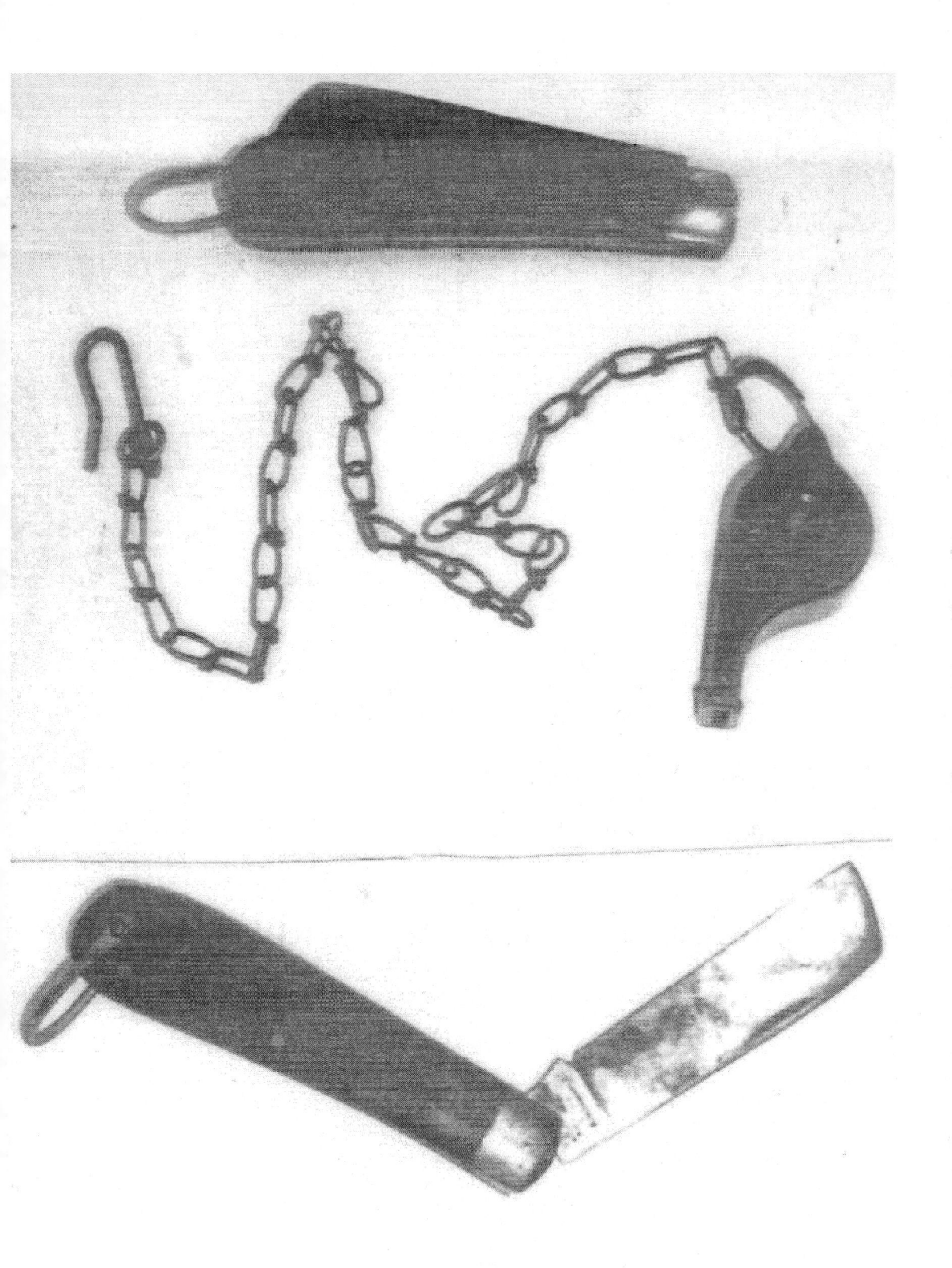

WHISTLE AND KNIFE

113 k

is on the surface, the lookout sees a spot of red in the distance. There is no knowledge of a freighter in those waters until this red spot appears and gives away the freighter's position. The submarine follows the freighter for six hours and at dawn torpedoes it. To satisfy his curiosity, the Captain questions the survivors. The light is a cigarette smoked on the bridge not by the man on watch but by another crewmember who just stops by for a chat.

The cruelty inflicted on the survivors of the S.S. Jean Nicolet and the other ships is terrible. What would happen if captured and imprisoned? Some of the P.O.W. (Prisoner of War) camps are found to be inhumane. The men in German camps are treated humanely, and are given medical treatment. The Germans, for the most part, followed the Rules of the Geneva Convention However, no man wants to be interned in a Japanese P.O. W. camp.

Stanley Willner is on the S.S.Sawokla when it is torpedoed in the Indian Ocean on November 19, 1942. Willner is so loaded with shrapnel that after he is picked up he spends two months in the German Cruiser Michel's hospital. After another month the Americans prisoners are turned over to the Japanese in Singapore. The first thing Willner does is to hand over his medical record the German doctor has given him. The Japanese response is to strike Willner with the broadside of his sword.

After a few months Willner and the other Americans are transferred from Singapore to one of Japan's most notorious camps. There they are starved and worked as slaves. One of the projects includes the Bridge Over the River Kwai. Willner weighs 135 pounds when he is first imprisoned. He drops to 75 pounds before he is released.

Willner is able to keep his good friend Dennis Roland, who is very sick, alive by stealing a duck. These men bribe a one-legged British soldier to hide the duck by giving him one egg each week. This poor one-legged Englishman accidentally overheats the Japanese bathwater. His punishment is to be boiled alive! Seamen Dennis Roland and Stanley Willner, somehow, managed to survive. How could a human watch another human be subjected to this kind of treatment? There can be no explanation for this conduct.

George Duffy is on the S.S. American Leader when the Cruiser Michel sinks her in September 1942. The 47 survivors (11 others are lost) are transferred to the Japanese. They at first have Korean guards. When the Japanese take them over, chaos reigns. At the end of the war British intelligence officers parachute into their camp and find that the prisoners are walking skeletons. Nineteen of the forty-seven survivors of the S.S. American Leader die during their Japanese imprisonment. Duffy is one of the survivors. He writes and lectures on the subject in the years to come.

Captured seamen are forced to work in coal mines, on construction projects and in planting rice. Their diet is rice, pickled radish, seaweed, and tea. Japanese P.O.W.'s are all treated cruelly and are given very little to eat.   Chapter 5 will detail the treatment the survivors receive upon their return to the United States at the end of World War II.

PROJECT IVORY SOAP

By the start of 1944 the war has moved from North Africa to across the Mediterranean. Allied troops invade Italy and Italian troops are assisting the Allies in pushing the Germans out of their country. Major planning for both the Northern European Invasion and the defeat of the Japanese is underway. The U.S.A. and its Allies are still a very long way from victory, and the road will be rough. Both the Germans and the Japanese become even tougher as the U.S. and its Allies approach their countries.

The Pacific War Theater is in a conventional mode with the U.S. planes and ground forces moving north island-to-island. To combat the Japanese Air Force a top secret project is planned. This project, "Ivory Soap", is so secret that it is not de-classified for over 50 years. The official history, <u>The Army Air Force in World War II</u>, makes no reference to this project.

Ivory Soap is officially approved and has 24 ships and 5,000 men from the army, navy, and Merchant Marine. The 24 ships have six Liberties and 18 180-foot freight/salvage (F/S) auxiliary vessels. The mission is to provide the facilities, shops, parts, and trained personnel to repair and maintain the B-19's and P-51's. Other planes can also be repaired as required. This project is assembled in Baltimore. When it is completed, it is moved to the Pacific.

The Army Transport Service (A.T.S.) operates the Liberties with all officers and men being Merchant Seamen. The Navy Armed Guard handles the guns. All ships are heavily armed with each Liberty having 334 man crews. Extra cannons and machine guns are added to each ship. Each ship is equipped with two motor launches and two "Ducks" (DUKW) and can accommodate two R-4B Sokorsky helicopters. The ducks, also called amphibians, can carry heavy loads on land or on water. Each of the six Liberties has its name changed to that of a General. The names are changed back after the war ends, but for now they are known as "The Generals".

In the Pacific conventional warfare depends on the B-29 bombers protected by the P-51. The enemy damages these planes and it is important that the planes making it back to base be repaired and put back in action. This is the goal of the Ivory Soap Project and it fulfills its mission.

This project is moved to the Pacific where it gives a good account of itself. A Memorial Plaque is, at a later date, dedicated in honor of this project. It is at the Air Force Museum at Dayton, Ohio (Top Project Ivory Soap———------ Air Craft Repair Ships http://www.usmm.org/felknorivory.html 1/10/2006).

Z-Men are seen wearing ribbons on their jackets and on their hats. They do not look like the ribbons other servicemen are wearing. These are Seamen wearing the citations that they have earned.

MERCHANT MARINE MEDALS AND RIBBONS

The United States decided to authorize citation awards to seamen. U.S. Merchant Marine medals differ from the medals awarded by the other services in that the authorization comes directly from the War Shipping Administration. If the Seaman is qualified for an award, he is issued a card with his name, the award, and a colored picture of the ribbon. Proof that the citation has been earned requires that a copy of the ship's discharge (See 118 1) for information directly from the ship to be presented. The citation award card is to be carried by the recipient at all times when he wears the ribbon or medal. This proves his right to wear the award. (See 118 1-2)

MERCHANT MARINE DISTINGUISHED SERVICE MEDAL

This is the highest award a seaman can receive. On or after September 3, 1939 a seaman must have performed outstanding conduct or service in the line of duty. Only one medal is issued with each similar citation awarded with an added suitable insignia.

MERCHANT MARINE MERITORIOUS SERVICE MEDAL

Any seaman whose conduct and service is outstanding but not of the level of Distinguished Service Medal performance is to receive this award.

MARINER MEDAL

Any seaman, who is wounded, injured or suffers exposure as a result of

SHIPS' DISCHARGES

EACH CREWMEMBER, WHEN PAID OFF AT THE COMPLETION OF THE VOYAGE, RECEIVES A SHIP'S DISCHARGE

SHIP'S DISCHARGE FOR A COASTWISE TRIP

SHIP'S DISCHARGE FOR A FOREIGN TRIP

WAR SHIPPING ADMINISTRATION

This is to certify that George E. Ward HAS BEEN AWARDED THE Pacific War Zone Bar confirming active service with THE UNITED STATES MERCHANT MARINE in that war area.

ADMINISTRATOR

WAR SHIPPING ADMINISTRATION

This is to certify that George E. Ward HAS BEEN AWARDED THE Mediterranean Middle East War Zone confirming active service with THE UNITED STATES MERCHANT MARINE in that war area.

U.S. DEPARTMENT OF TRANSPORTATION
MARITIME ADMINISTRATION

This is to certify that GEORGE E. WARD HAS BEEN AWARDED by the War Shipping Administration the Philippine Liberation Ribbon confirming active service with THE UNITED STATES MERCHANT MARINE in that war area.

FORM MA-881-J
Maritime Administrator

WAR SHIPPING ADMINISTRATION

This is to certify that George E. Ward HAS BEEN AWARDED THE Atlantic War Zone Bar confirming active service with THE UNITED STATES MERCHANT MARINE in that war area.

U.S. DEPARTMENT OF TRANSPORTATION
MARITIME ADMINISTRATION

This is to certify that GEORGE E. WARD HAS BEEN AWARDED by the War Shipping Administration the **The Merchant Marine Combat Bar** confirming active service with THE UNITED STATES MERCHANT MARINE in a ship which was engaged in direct enemy action.

FORM MA-881-G
Maritime Administrator

U.S. DEPARTMENT OF TRANSPORTATION
MARITIME ADMINISTRATION

This is to certify that GEORGE E. WARD, JR. HAS BEEN AWARDED BY THE WAR SHIPPING ADMINISTRATION the **VICTORY MEDAL** confirming active service with THE UNITED STATES MERCHANT MARINE or MARITIME SERVICE during WORLD WAR II.

MA 881B (10-81)
Captain Warren G. Le
Maritime Administrator

enemy action receives this medal. In the event of death the medal is presented to the recipient named on his insurance policy..

PRISONER OF WAR MEDAL

Any Merchant Seaman held as a prisoner of war between December 7, 1941 and August 15, 1945 is entitled to this medal (For a photo of these citations see p. 119 m).

GALLANT SHIP CITATION

All officers and crewmembers are given this citation. The ship is also presented a Gallant Ship plaque which is placed on the ship. Only nine of these citations are awarded.

PHILIPPINE DEFENSE RIBBON

This is awarded to all seaman serving 30 days or more in Philippine waters from December 8, 1941 to June 15, 1942.

PHILIPPINE LIBERATION RIBBON

All seamen serving in Philippine waters for no less than 30 days from October 17, 1944 to September 3, 1945 are eligible for this ribbon.

COMBAT BAR

This is awarded to a seaman who serves on a ship that is attacked or damaged by an instrument of war and/or abandoned. For a ship that the Seaman must abandon, a star is attached. One additional star is authorized for each

U.S. MERCHANT MARINE CITATIONS AND AWARDS

Merchant Marine Service Emblem

Honorable Service Button

- Distinguished Service Medal 
- Meritorious Service Medal 
- Mariners Medal 
- Prisoner of War Medal

- Combat Bar 
- Philippine Defense Ribbon 
- Philippine Liberation Ribbon 
- Guardian 9-11 Ribbon 
- Gallant Ship Ribbon

- Atlantic War Zone Medal
- Mediterranean-Middle East War Zone Medal 
- Pacific War Zone Medal 
- Victory Medal 
- Defense Medal

abandonment. There will be a medal authorized for every Merchant Marine Bar awarded with the exception of the Combat bar. No explanation is offered for the Combat bar not having a medal. (See photo p 119 m for the above four awards.)

MERCHANT MARINE DEFENSE MEDAL

This medal is awarded for service in the Merchant Marine before Pearl Harbor. All crewmembers who serve from September 8, 1939 to December 7, 1941 receive this medal.

ATLANTIC WAR ZONE BAR, MEDITERRANEAN-MIDDLE EAST WAR ZONE BAR, AND PACIFIC WAR ZONE BAR

This Citations are for Seamen who serve in each of these three war zones for 30 days or more.

VICTORY MEDAL

This Citation is for crewmembers who serve 30 days or more December 7, 1941 to September 3, 1945(See photo of this award p119 m).

In addition to the above awards, each seaman who serves 30 days or more December 7, 1941 to September 3, 1945 receives an Honorable Service Button and a Merchant Marine Service Emblem (Merchant Marine Emblems, Medals and Ribbons http:www.usmm.org/medals.html). The purchase of the medal is the responsibility of each Seaman. Medals and ribbons are sold by a number of companies. Miniature medals are available for civilian dress wear. Enameled Metal Pins are also available for Armed Forces caps.

Ship explosions are thought of as a tragedy that happens at sea or in a foreign country. Usually true, but they also strike right here in the U.S.A. In the San Francisco area when a ship docks at Port Chicago everyone knows that the cargo, at least in part, is ammunition. When a ship goes to Port Chicago a Seaman, knowing this danger, may decide to leave the ship if he has not already signed the Articles. Very few leave. Most elect to make the voyage.

The Liberty Ship, The S.S. E.A. Bryan and the Victory ship, The S.S. Quinault Victory are docked at Port Chicago on July 17, 1944. The Bryan is being loaded with ammunition when it explodes. The Quinault is also loading ammunition that is set off in a chain reaction. Both ships are blown into little pieces and 67 Merchant Seamen are vaporized. The little town of Little Chicago is leveled and vessel pieces fly as far as two miles away. On the two ships alone, counting the gun crew members, 110 men are killed. The number of longshoremen and stevedores lost makes this incident extremely sad, as this kind of accident is not expected in the U.S.

The Ivory Soap Project is performing its mission in the South Pacific. The U.S. Army and our Allies are moving north into Italy, and the U.S. Navy and the U. S. Marines are taking control in the Pacific. Now the time approaches for the big Invasion everyone is waiting for. There is no doubt that the U. S. and its Allies will strike across the English Channel. The Germans know this and are preparing for it, although many of their forces are busy on the Eastern Front with the U.S.S.R.

D--DAY NORMANDY INVASION

General Eisenhower and his staff are preparing for the largest invasion the world has ever seen. Ships are assembling in the British Isles by the hundreds. Every type of warship, tanker, landing craft, tug boat, Merchant Ship, etc. is there. The invasion forces are ready to go at exactly the right time to the right location and everything is coordinated correctly in time with the weather.

It is D-Day June 6, 1944. The Invasion of Normandy begins. The first assault has 160,000 men with 16,000 vehicles They fight from the sea to the beaches attempting to secure control. There are 13,000 aircraft, which includes 5,000 fighters, 400 bombers and 3,500 gliders. 4,000 landing ships of every description accompany this force—over 200 are Liberties. This is the largest number of Naval and Merchant ships ever amassed.

The Liberties have different responsibilities. Some will shuttle back and forth from England bringing in more men and supplies. Others, unfortunately, will be sunk. For some their fate is already scheduled. They are not going to return. They are to perform a special task. These Liberties perform a duty which will save countless lives. These plans go by the codenames of Gooseberry and Mulberry 'A" (American).

GOOSEBERRY   This is the codename for a plan to sink a line of ships to form a block shelter. These ships are sunk in 2 ½ fathoms of water (15 feet) to provide a breakwater. The Liberties used for this project have all suffered war damage prior to D-Day. "Utah" and "Omaha" beaches are designated as the sites for Gooseberry 1 and 2. These two sites, after much study, are selected as the most favorable in assisting the invading troops for protection from the Germans and from the weather.

A terrific battle is raging when the first three Liberties go into Utah. These three are scuttled in place. The first Liberties going into Omaha are not as lucky. The first in, The S.S. George S. Wasson, is hit by a shell and then a German bomber blows up over her deck. Tugs cannot tow her against the tide and she sinks out of position. The next Liberty, The S.S. Matt W. Ransom, attempts to move into the position where the Wasson was to be placed. She is damaged while under dive-bomber attack and she cannot be controlled. She drifts over one thousand feet and sinks in shallow water. The third Liberty, The S.S. Benjamin Conter, is under heavy attack and is cut loose by the tugs. Under her own power she takes her position. The other Liberties settle in position and the breakwater is complete. The two ships that drift away have smaller craft take connecting positions and two smaller harbors are formed. These breakwaters are used for mooring Liberty supply ships.

Huge floating caissons (Phoenixes) are towed from England. A total of 75 Phoenixes are put into operation. These artificial harbors are big enough to handle seven Liberties. Also constructed are floating roads and rail tracks. This project is on a time schedule that requires considerable coordination. The tug boats are extremely important and they do their jobs.

MULBERRY 'A' (AMERICAN) The Mulberry is the code name given to an artificial harbor to be constructed in Normandy. It is created for landing stores and ammunition at the invasion beaches. The construction time is estimated at thirty days. Under extremely adverse conditions the beach is completed in just ten days. Some of the worst weather in years comes after the construction.

This project is considered one of the greatest maritime engineering feats in history. Admiral Sir Bertram H Ramsey, Allied Naval Commander-In-Chief, decorates the ten tugboat captains and complimented every Merchant Seaman who participated.

So many Liberties make so many shuttles back and forth across the English Channel that it is given a nickname. It is now called Liberty Lane. This is the largest collection of Liberties ever assembled.

The Normandy Invasion is successful. The United States and its Allies are now firmly established and the Germans are pushed back. More fighting troops, equipment, ammunition, and supplies must be delivered before victory is declared. The Liberties are there delivering the goods.

The war is going much better now. The Russians are pushing the Germans back and they are retaking their country. The U.S. forces are moving north in the Pacific taking possession of the islands away from the Japanese. Allied forces are moving toward Germany.

Life aboard a Liberty is a little less hectic than when the young United States Maritime Trainee first goes aboard a ship. He is now an Oiler or a Fireman/ Water Tender if he is a member of the Black (engine) Gang. He receives his A.B. rating and possibly even ships out as a Bosun in the Deck Department. If he is in the Steward Department he is possibly the Chief Cook. He has been home several times and does not wear a uniform unless he wants to. When he elects to wear civilian clothes, he hears remarks such as "slacker" or "draft dodger". A lady point blank asks, "Why aren't you in the service? My son is." He may elect to just walk away. He may show her his Atlantic or Pacific War Zone Bar Card and his Combat Card with a star for the ship he lost, which sank with 22 of his fellow shipmates. The response to this action if often just silence. In some cases the Z-Man opens his shirt and shows her a chest with nothing but scars suffered when a bomb hit his ship starting a raging fire. Now the nosy woman is embarrassed. As a Z-Man he gets used to this treatment. One of the best retorts was made by O.S. Don Pearson at Eureka, Utah. Home after the invasion at Ewo Jima, Don has an acquaintance who is on a U.S. Navy cruiser also at the invasion. The young sailor is a hero and he delights in letting everyone he knows where he has been. He finally goes too far and belittles Don calling him a draft dodger. Don then tells this sailor, whose name and ship shall remain silent, that he was also at Ewo Jima. He tells this loudmouth that his cruiser was anchored 10 miles out shelling the island, while Don's Liberty was at the beach in the thick of the fighting. Said in front of a number of people this is the perfect squelch.

Back on the ship he feels at home. Traveling to Scotland or England is old stuff. He knows his way around. He may know a girl or have a favorite pub. It is much better now. There are fewer air raids. If he is in the Pacific his Liberty ship probably goes south to New Guinea or Northern Australia before heading north. This is the safest route for most Merchant Ships to follow. Enroute to the South Pacific the Liberty again crosses the International Date Line. Explanation of the I.D.L sounds clear and simple. Meridian, Greenwich and Longitudes when mixed become very complicated. Finally the answer is, a day is lost which is regained on the return trip.

In Port Moresby he already knows the story about the topless native women. A Chaplain, upset about the native women not wearing tops, issues a large number of under shirts to the ladies to try to remedy the situation. To his dismay he discovers the next day that round holes have been cut in areas –allowing the ladies to go unencumbered.

If he stops for the first time at Darwin, he learns that Australians think this is the area the Japanese will most likely invade. The Japanese have hit the town hard. Every building has damage from minor to complete destruction. All civilians have been evacuated. Barbed wire is strung and the Aussies are ready. With the civilians evacuated only limited entertainment is available. The Red Cross and the Salvation Army set up tents and coffee and doughnuts are served. A talent contest is organized. The few ships in port and the local Aussie Military Detachment each enter an act. Everybody enjoys the vocal groups, a tap dancer a yodeler, a banjo player, and a harmonica player. There are only a few nurses stationed in Darwin. None have any trouble finding dates.

Darwin has a beautiful beach. Many take a swim and/or lie in the sun. Some of the swimmers will have to be treated for an ear fungus infection at the next port. This fungus is not serious—just 10 minutes with eardrops and the fungus is gone. The doctors, before the seaman says anything, will tell him that he has been swimming in the North Australian water. They evidently see many of these cases.

The Merchant Seamen are once again at sea. Occasionally a flying fish sails over the rail on to the deck. He flops around on deck until a seaman catches him and throws him back into the ocean. An albatross lands on the ship. He flaps his wings but is unable to take off. The big bird's wings are too long and it is impossible for him to get enough air under them to take off. Two of the crew approach the bird and he doesn't try to resist their approach. Each man places one hand under the body and one hand under a wing. They gently lift the big bird so the wings can function. The albatross flies off a little way and then returns to within six feet of the men. It's almost as if he is saying "Thank you." Lines are put out and several big fish are caught. There is fresh fish for dinner. These fish weigh well over 100 lbs. each.

There is a report of an enemy submarine in the area where the ship is heading. As the ship is sailing alone (not in convoy) the course is immediately changed to avoid possible dangers. A mine is spotted by the lookout. The ship stops and the gun crew springs into action. The mine is on the port side; therefore the sailors on the port side get some 20 MM practice. Many shots are fired. The mine does not explode but is definitely hit a number of times as indicated by the tracers. Is it a dud? No one knows. So many rounds penetrate the mine that it fills with water and sinks. A ship may have been saved. At least this mine is no longer a menace.

For exercise the crewmembers walk up and down the deck when the weather is not bad. It is fun to watch the porpoises flitting back and forth at the ship's bow. They are a delight to watch. There are stories that unconscious seamen floating in lifejackets have been nudged into shore by porpoises. It may be true or it may just be a "sea story".

Another American Liberty passes. The seaman is washing clothes the way he is taught by an old seaman. He slices a bar of soap into slivers and puts them in a bucket of water with the steam pipe extending into it. The water becomes extremely hot. Clothes are added and the agitation is performed with a plunger. Little primitive, but it works.

Someone yells, "Come and see the whales." Everyone not on watch takes in this wonderful experience of seeing 30 or more whales. Elementary school lessons remind the seaman that whales are not fish but are mammals. Is this large number of magnificent sea animals called a herd?

One A.B. is a boxer. John Szeliga of Philadelphia makes a heavy punching bag. He trains with another seaman who has a little ring experience. He stays in shape and continues to work hard. After the war John goes on to become the 160 pound amateur champion in Philadelphia.

Life is not easy going for the soldiers and marines. These courageous men are fighting enemies who are dug in. They no longer are attempting to conquer other countries but are fighting hard to keep their own country from being over run.

The Russians continue to advance toward Germany. The Americans and Allies are moving in for a last German stand. What is soon to take place is the biggest battle the world has every experienced. It is fought under very cold conditions against a very determined enemy. It is known forever as the "Battle of the Bulge". In the end the Allies prevail, but at what a price. The number of fighting men involved in this battle is astounding.

The Battle of the Bulge starts on December 16, 1944 and ends on January 25, 1945. The numbers tell the story.. There are 600,000 Americans and 55,000 British battling 500,000 Germans. American causalities alone are 81,000 including 19,000 killed. The Germans suffer 100,000 casualties. This battle lasts less than six weeks.

In March 1945 following the Battle of the Bulge the Allies smash through the Siegfried Line and cross the Rhine. After overrunning Western Germany the Allies meet with the Russian Army and Germany collapses. Hitler and Eva Braun, whom he has just married, commit suicide. The unconditional surrender is signed at Rheims on May 7, 1945.

VICTORY IN EUROPE

Victory is finally achieved in Europe officially on May 8, 1945 –V E Day. While the war still rages in the Pacific there is much to be accomplished in Europe. Germany is divided into four sectors. The U.S.A., Britain, France, or the U.S.S.R. each control one sector. For the serviceman who has survived the Battle of the Bulge or any other battles, this is good news—bad news or good news—good news.

The good news—bad news falls on those men who are going to be returned to the U.S.A. The good news is that the war in Europe is now over and they are still alive. They go on leave and spend some time at home. The bad news is after their leaves they will be sent to the Pacific War Theater to fight the Japanese. This is not a bright future for these veterans.

The good news—good news is that for some the European war is over. It is also good news that they remain in Europe in the Army of Occupation. They do not have to go to the Pacific to fight the Japanese. They bring their wives and children over and resume a more normal living.

They look forward to the Occupational Duty. Mainly in Germany, Austria, and France where there are Army and Army Air Force Personnel. In Italy the Army and Navy are in control. Housing is being constructed for military personnel. Homes are requisitioned for Headquarters and troop facilities. All the requirements for a military occupation i.e. Post Exchange, service clubs, movies, libraries, snack bars. etc. are satisfied. The military dependents are coming, and they require a school system with teacher and educational facilities. The Liberty Ships are converted for transporting the dependents, their belongings, and all the equipment and supplies needed for the Occupation. The Liberties are also transporting war brides to the U.S.

While the Battle of the Bulge is raging the U.S. Marines are taking possession of the islands the Japanese control. The Americans pay dearly for this worthless real estate, but they do their duties. One of the bloodiest and most terrible actions is to take place at Tarawa. The U.S. Navy does its job of shelling the beach to assist the Marines in their landing. The Army Air Corps accomplishes all it can in softening up the Japanese with bombs. This proves to be very inadequate, however.

The order to move in is given and the U.S. Marines hit the beach. It is a slaughter. Even with all the advance action the Japanese resistance is extremely strong. The first wave results in 90% casualties. The second wave hits the beach and 50% are casualties. Finally the third wave goes in and there is still a 20% casualty rate. The island is taken but a terrible price is paid. This invasion results, percentage-wise, in one of the worst U.S. Marine casualty rates ever suffered.

Some of the U.S. Marines and the U.S. Army Servicemen are in more than one invasion. Some are in three or more. The Liberty Ship is in every one assisting these courageous men. Still ahead are some very big targets. The Philippines must be retaken. Japan must be defeated on its own shores on the land and in the cities. The U.S. Merchant Marine is busy bringing in more men, equipment, and supplies. The job is still far from over. In the U.S.A. the U.S. Maritime Service is still trying to attract trainees. Men are needed in the Merchant Marine. The recruiting offices are working to find recruits. Ads are posted. Uncle Sam is still pointing his finger and saying, "I NEED YOU". The Z-Men, although now experienced, are constantly cautioned not to talk about ship loadings, destinations, etc.(See photos p. 132 n,o).

UNCLE SAM POSTER

RECRUITMENT POSTERS

The American and Allied Forces move into the Philippines. Philippine Guerrillas, who are waiting for the opportunity for revenge, are now paying the Japanese back for the cruelty they inflicted on the Philippine people. General MacArthur fulfills his pledge to the Philippine people that he will return, and he does return!

The Liberty Ship in the Pacific is traveling, as required, under blackout. The Radio Officer comes to the mess halls and reads a bulletin. The U.S. has dropped a large bomb on a town in Japan. He says the whole town is burning. Every man stands and cheers. Now the speculation starts. "It must have been a super bomb." "It had to be a much larger bomb than normal". One Naval Gunner has the idea that everyone agrees is probably correct. He says that the Japanese homes are made of bamboo or other types of wood. Therefore it must be a large incendiary bomb to start all the reported fires. This sounds logical. This terrific bomb is dropped on August 6, 1945.

Three days later the crew is still talking about the big bomb that is dropped on a Japanese city. The Radio Operator again comes to the mess hall with a bulletin. Another big bomb is dropped on a different city. Now the speculation turns to whether or not this leads to the end of the war. Some think that it will; others think the Japanese are so fanatic that they will fight to the end.

Later the Radio Operator informs the crew that the bombs are Atomic Bombs. No one has ever heard of an Atomic Bomb. Is it a bigger bomb? Is it super loaded? Every crewmember agrees to one thing. This bomb is something that may get us all home sooner.

A few days later bulletins tell the crew that these super bombs have names. The first is named "Little Boy". Army Colonel Tibbets carries "Little Boy" in a plane named after his mother, Enola Gay. Not many people remember the names of the American planes, but this one will be long remembered because of its great importance in history. Colonel Tibbet pilots the Enola Gay toward the target while the bomb is being armed by Navy Captain William Parsons. Arming is done during the flight to reduce possible dangers at take off. After a six-hour flight to Hiroshima, Captain Tibbet releases "Little Boy". It explodes about 2,000 feet over the city center. Up to 80,000 people die instantly and many more die later from exposure to this bomb. This is the first nuclear bomb in history. By December of 1945 an estimated total of 145,000 people die.

Hiroshima is selected as a target by the U.S.A. because it is a city with a vast amount of industrial and military importance. It has not been touched by bombs and this is an ideal area for study of the atom bomb's destructive power.. It is thought not to have any American or Allied Prisoners of War housed there. Sadly it is learned later that there are 11 Americans killed by the bomb. There is also a number of Japanese-Americans from the U.S.A. who die.

The second atomic bomb with the code name "Fat Man" follows the same basic procedure as "Little Boy". The original target is Kokura, but weather conditions require the secondary target of Nagasaki to be the second victim.. Nagasaki is selected as it is one of Japan's largest seaports in the south and is a large industrial center. It is an important military complex. It is estimated that 74,000 people die from the explosion and after effects. Will this be enough to influence the Japanese to give up?

There is great joy on the Liberties and all ships with both Navy and Merchant Seamen celebrating. No one knows but it is the hoped that Japan is now ready to surrender and this ship and crew can go home. It is wonderful to think that there are no worries about submarines, mines, or Kamikazes. Every one is now bothering the Radio Officers for the latest news about the war. The bulletins continue to come in, but the ship is still not breaking radio silence; thus there are many questions that cannot be asked.

The introduction and effect of these two atomic bombs is hard to imagine for men on a Liberty Ship out on the ocean. This is all the crew talks about and the possibility of going home. No one can ever remember a bomb being given a name. Everyone agrees that this is payback for the times a ship's crewmembers make it safely to a lifeboat when a torpedo sinks their ship only to be machine gunned to death. This lets the Japanese know about the terror coming from above like when a Kamikaze slams into an American ship. This is revenge for the ships and men who suffered and died in the Japanese sneak attack on Pearl Harbor.

There is no compassion for the Japanese. They are our enemy. This is payback time and the crew is savoring this news.

While the planning and preparation for the Atomic Bombs has been taking place, U.S. Forces are busy in the Pacific. They are moving ever closer to Japan. The Philippines are, at present, controlled by U.S. and Allied troops. All the way through the Liberties are there. When General Douglas MacArthur is forced to leave the Philippines, he said those famous well-known words "I will return". Now that he has returned, what does he say about the men of the U.S. Merchant Marine, the Z-Men? "I wish to commend to you the valor of the Merchant Seamen participating with us in the liberation of the Philippines. With us they have shared the heaviest enemy fire. On this island I have ordered them off their ships and into foxholes when their ships became untenable targets of attack. At our side they have suffered in bloodshed and in death. The high caliber of efficiency and courage they displayed in their part of the invasion of the Philippines marked their conduct throughout the entire campaign in the southwest Pacific area. They have contributed tremendously to our success. I hold no branch in higher esteem than the Merchant Marine Service" (The United States at War 1946 p.32).

The Liberty Ship crew is now a little more relaxed. The prevailing thought is maybe the Japanese will surrender and the U.S. won't have to make that invasion. No one wants to have to face a determined dug-in Japanese invasion defense.

The crew is, at present, looking forward to the end of the war. Everyone is, of course, a little older and certainly much more mature. Maritime Service Training is just a memory. The seaman is now an A.B. and a real Z-Man. The old 78 records on the hand crank record player are getting a little worn. The songs, which were popular when he left the States, are probably not on the "Hit Parade" anymore. The stories and jokes are getting stale. Someone says, " Do you remember this one?" As the ship is going down and seamen are getting into the lifeboats the Captain asks, "Anyone here know how to pray?" One crewmember steps forward and says, "I know how to pray." "Good" says the Captain, "You pray while the rest of us put on our lifejackets. We are one short." This is an old joke and most of the crewmembers have heard it.

Most men think back to being in high school just a short time back. Since then they have been to places the history teacher talked about and they now know first hand. Many think of the girl back home. Some receive a "Dear John" letter telling them she has decided to marry a guy she dated before him. Some return to the U.S.A. and marry the girl back home and "swallow the anchor". Swallow the anchor! Now he knows that term. It simply means that he quits the Merchant Marine and stops being a seaman. For some it is just the opposite. They have found a love for the sea and it becomes their life's occupation.

Whatever their thoughts are all are happy they have not "crossed over the bar" That is another expression they've learned. To "cross over the bar" means to die or to be killed. While every seaman knows the expression many do not know its origin. Former Z-Man A.B. Edward "Ed" Dierkes explains" .....When a seaman " crosses over the bar", we never say he died or passed way. We say he or she "crossed over the bar" or "passed over the bar". A bar is a ridge of sand built up by currents especially in a rivers or coastal waterways. The Merchant Marine dates back to 1775, the days of Privateers, when sea captains owned their ships before the Revolutionary War. Before our country had a military. Even before dredges were invented to keep the waterways clear........" (Dierkes, 2006)

The seaman's thoughts go to his crewmembers who have "crossed over the bar". Even though the friendship is only for six months, the tie is close. Within the confines of a ship 441.6 feet long men work together, eat together, sleep in the same foscle, etc. for 24 hours a day, 7 days a week—except for brief shore leaves. Even when time is spent ashore it's usually with the same men. When seamen learn an old shipmate goes down with the ship, there is a void on their next trip. Seamen are realists. While they miss that friend, they think, "I could have been on that Liberty".

Then it happens. Coming off watch and stretched out on his bunk the seaman hears a roar. Something's happened! He jumps up and enters the passageway. Every one is yelling. "The Japs are surrendering!' What the world has been waiting for since December 7, 1941 has finally happened. Have they really surrendered, or is it just another rumor?

What happens now? Nothing. No one trusts the Japanese. The Liberty continues as always i.e. lookouts are diligent, as ever, and the ship continues under blackout. Everyone is hopeful but remains patient. Soon the ship can really relax. The Japanese are going to meet with General MacArthur on the Battleship Missouri to sign the proper surrender documents. Care must be taken. Although planes and submarines are no longer a danger, there are still mines out there. No one wants any problems now.

Now what happens? The Liberty proceeds to her destination and the cargo is unloaded. The gun crew shakes hands with everyone and departs the ship. Two gunners remain to care for the guns. The reason the gun crew is taken off is that the ship is not going back to the U.S.A. yet. The gunners all wonder when they will be shipped home. They would rather stay on the Liberty because they think they may have a long wait for a place on a troop ship. The Liberty might just beat them home. It is going to Australia to pick up a cargo of wool and some war brides.

The Liberty is loaded; the war brides are quartered in the focsles formerly used by the gun crew. This is not first class travel, but the ladies are anxious to get to the U.S.A. and their husbands. It's a long sea trip from Australia to the U.S., but the Liberty makes it.

There is no "Welcome home greeting" when the Liberty docks. There is no band playing. There are no dignitaries to greet the seamen and make speeches of appreciation. That's all right with the seamen. The documents are signed on the Battleship Missouri on V J Day, September 2, 1945. THEY ARE GOING HOME AND THE WAR IS OVER!!

CHAPTER FIVE

POST WAR II MERCHANT MARINE

THE LIBERTY SHIP

It is often said that the Missouri mules won World War I when the mechanized vehicles were bogged down in the mud. Likewise, it is said, that the Liberty Ships won World War II. A better statement probably is that WWII could not have been won without the Liberty Ships or some similar type vessels. No one can argue that the Liberty Ships didn't do the job for which they were created.

The first Liberty Ship built was the S.S. Patrick Henry. She was built on September 27, 1941. The last one, launched on September 26, 1945 was the S.S. Albert M. Boie. In this four-year span the world had never before seen such a shipbuilding frenzy. The shipbuilders, Henry J. Kaiser being the best known, with their men and women employees built a total of 2,710 Liberty Ships during this period. These Liberties did the job for which they were intended.

They took part in every invasion hauling men and supplies. Almost 8½%, a total of 229, were sunk by enemy action—with 50 sunk on their maiden voyages. An indication of how dangerous certain areas were is the 12½ % loss of all U.S. Merchant Ships that were going to Russia in 1942. Most of these losses were on the very dangerous Murmansk run.

In addition to the 229 Liberties sunk by enemy action, there were the 61 that broke in half. Some others ran aground and broke into pieces. There were the Liberties that were an invaluable part of the Goosebury and The Mulberry Projects. These project ships, already damaged by enemy action, were scuttled to form breakwaters and artificial harbors, thus saving countess American and Allied lives. Many Liberties were sold to foreign countries. Some twenty-seven years later become artificial fish reefs. The rest are to remain in the laid up reserve fleet until they go to the shipbreakers for scrapping. Only two survive as viable ships.

What happens to some of these ships before they end up with the shipbreakers is an interesting story. In order to make them more profitable, they must be capable of carrying a larger load. This is accomplished by making them longer; thus supplying more cargo space. From 441'6" she is lengthened to 511'6". This alteration is completed in at least three different shipyards--all in foreign countries. Those converted were the Liberty Ship Tankers. Evidently the same blueprints were used at the different shipyards.

One ship, that is thought to be the last Liberty in commercial use, is the S.S. Ross C. Marvin. She was launched in November 29, 1943 and she was loaned to the British under the Lend Lease Program. Later she was sold to China and her name was changed three different times. This Liberty operated until 1987 when she went to the Chinese shipbreakers and was scrapped.

The enemy in WWII captured not one Liberty. The Navy's instruction to the ships' Captains was to never let the ship fall into enemy hands. The Master was to use every means possible to prevent this from happening. He was to use his guns to the fullest and to use ship maneuverability to the limit. If capture became inevitable every means was to be taken to beach or scuttle the ship. Many ships were set on fire or deliberately sunk, but not one was captured.

THE Z-MEN GO HOME

The war is over and crewmembers are ready to head for home. When the ship docks back in the U.S. A., the seaman receives his final pay off and is given his ship's discharge. He shakes hands with his shipmates and leaves the ship. He catches a train for home and looks forward to the future. Some will marry and resume old jobs. Some are ready to seek employment; others plan to continue their education, which had been interrupted.

These are all volunteers. Some are under the (draft) Selective Service age of 18 when they join the U.S. Maritime Service. Some are too old for the draft. Many have handicaps and are 4F, which means that none of the other services can use them. They are told that they are required to have 32 months of sea time in order to qualify for a "Statement of Substantial Continuous Service in the United States Merchant Marine". This 32-month time requirement is shortened to 14 months. This qualifies the Z-Man for an 1-G Selective Service Classification which is the equivalent of the Honorably Discharged Veterans 1-C classification issued by the Selective Service

There is no GI Bill for the Z-Man that will pay his way through college. There is no VA home loan to assist him with lower interest rates in purchasing a home. The Veterans Organizations, such as the V.F.W. (Veterans of Foreign Wars) and the American Legion, do not accept him as a member. Should he apply for a government job, he is not granted extra points for his service time. All of the other services are granted these points.

The non-acceptance by Veterans' groups is a joke. The local chapters and posts welcome and accept the Z–Men, but the national hierarchy says, "No". In a few cases the seamen actually are elected and serve as Commanders or Presidents of the local groups. If the National Headquarters becomes aware of this situation, they order the local posts to have these men resign or be ousted. Consider this ridiculous situation. The seamen are good enough to be the heads of the organizations but are not good enough to be members. To remedy these situations the local organizations, in some cases, change the seamen's status to Honorary Memberships. This gives them all the benefits of a full membership except the right to vote or hold office, and they pay <u>no dues</u>.

SEAMEN'S PAY

The argument has always been made by the National Veterans Organizations, especially the V.F.W., that seamen made big salaries compared to the other servicemen. This argument shall now be compared from both sides:

<u>NEGATIVE VIEW</u>—Seamen made bigger salaries than the other services—no argument they did (Refer to page 71-72). Seamen received bonuses that the other services did not receive. No argument, they did (Refer to page 72).

POSITIVE VIEW---Pay periods.---The pay stopped (completely) when the seamen signed off the ship and did not start again until they returned to a ship.

TRAVEL PAY---The seamen has no transportation or per diem when going to their homes or going to the ports where they are next to be assigned to a ship.

ILLNESS REQUIRING SEAMEN TO LEAVE SHIP---The seamen no longer receives pay, as they are no longer on the ship.

ABANDON SHIP SITUATION--- The seamen no longer receives pay, as they are no longer on the ship.

LIFEBOAT OR LIFE RAFT--- The seamen no longer receives pay, as they are no longer on the ship.

HOSPITAL STAY AFTER LIFEBOAT CRISES--- The seamen no longer receives pay, as they no longer are on the ship.

MUSTERING OUT PAY---This pay is awarded all servicemen except the seamen. The seamen do not receive any remuneration.

P.O.W. (Prisoner of war) ---Seamen receive no pay during confinement.

KILLED OR INJURED---Seamen can receive treatment in a Marine hospital for injuries suffered aboard ship but they receive no pay during confinement. A maximum of $5,000.00 is paid the seamen's families in event of death. All other servicemen's families receive $10,000.00.

G I BILL---This bill is for education and vocational training after discharge. All services except seamen receive this. The seamen do not qualify.

V A HOME LOANS ---All other services qualify. The seamen do not qualify.

The difference between a Merchant Seaman's family receiving $5,000.00 and all other servicemen's families getting $10,000.00 is referred to as The Five Thousand Dollar Solution. By early 1942 all private shipping company ships are under the control of the U.S. Government. Seamen are now working for the U.S. Government and should be considered federal employees. All federal employees are eligible for workers compensation benefits under F.E.C.A.(Federal Employees Compensation Act).

In 1943 the U.S. Government passes a bill that Seamen are not to be considered as officers or employees of the United States. This prevents Seamen from filing F.E.C.A. claims and there is no place to seek compensation. There are no death benefits for parents, siblings, or if married, widows and orphans.

All Seamen are then given a $5,000.00 insurance policy. This insurance is to cover every contingency up to a maximum of $5,000.00. The payments are to be made monthly at the seamen's pay rate. For instance, if an Oiler earns $100.00 per month is blinded for life in an explosion, he receives $100.00 per month until $5,000.00 has been paid. If he is killed, his beneficiary receives the same. If an Ordinary Seaman loses a leg, he receives $82.50 a month. This is less than a soldier, who never leaves the states, receives while attending college on the G I Bill.

After the war in June of 1947 the Senate declares this program had ended six months after the war ended. Other services pay lifetime disabilities, pensions, and dependency benefits. The dependency benefits are paid to the widow until she remarries and to the children up to age 18.

The Marshall Plan aided our former enemies, their widows, and children "....The men who slaughtered and maimed the Merchant Mariners were treated better, as were their widows and orphans, than the U.S. Merchant Seamen or their survivors" (Dooley "American Merchant Marine Veterans News" Spring 2006 p 18).

Now the complete comparison has been made. There is no question as to which services profit the most. One example must be made considering the pay situation. The story of P.O.W. Stanley Willner (p. 116-117) has been told, but his pay situation has not. Willner's ship the S.S. Sawokla is torpedoed on November 29, 1942 and he is a P.O.W. until the war ended. Not knowing that he is still alive, the U.S. government pays Willner's family $1.00 per day since his disappearance. When the government finds out that he is still alive, what do you think happened? The federal government wants the Willner family to reimburse the government the meager sum that is being paid to them. You be the judge as to the fairness of this directive. Remember Willner receives no pay for the three years of his imprisonment as a PO.W. Willner loses 60 pounds from his original 135 pounds by the time he is released from the P.O.W Camp. Willner is one of only 400 alive out of 1,600 at the Japanese Prison Camp at Kwai, Thailand. He makes it back to the United States weighing only 75 lbs. and without one-penny pay. Do you think that he is able to locate and fulfill the duties of a job?

Z-MEN KILLED

The facts concerning pay cannot be concluded without comparing the numbers of men killed in the different services. The exact number of Z-Men killed is difficult to determine because some American Seamen ship out on our Allies' Merchant Ships. The most in depth research is conducted by Captain Arthur R. Moore, author of "A Careless Word –A Needless Sinking: A History of the Staggering Losses Suffered by The U.S. Merchant Marine Both In Ship and Personnel During World War II." His figures are used for this study.

The Merchant Marine has 243,000 men who serve in WWII. There are various totals given by different sources, but the figure used here is from the War Shipping Administration, release on January 1, 1946. The number of USMM killed is 9,512 or 1 in 26. (3.90%). This causality rate is much higher than that of the Marine Corps. The Marine Corps has 669,108 men with 19,733 killed or 1 in 34 (2.94%). The Army totals include the Army Air Corps as the U.S. Air Force is established later. The Army has 11,268,000 men of which 234,874 die or a ratio of 1 in 48 (2.08%). The Navy has 4,183,466 men with 36,958 dying or a ratio of 1 in 114. (0.88%). The Coast Guard proves to be the safest service with 574 killed out of 242,093 for a ratio of 1-421 0.24%)(American Merchant Marine Casualties http://usmm.org/casualty.html).

Along with the Seamen who lose their lives, 1,810 Navy Armed Guard Sailors make the supreme sacrifice. Of all the different Navy units the Armed Guard has one of the highest death percentages.

The different citations earned by Merchant Seamen (p 119) are a mirror of the action he encounters in every war theater. The Meritorious Service Medal has a total of 424 recipients. This is the highest award a Seaman can receive.

Service in the Atlantic War Zone for 30 days earns 235,298 Seamen this war zone ribbon. A total of 150,184 Mediterranean- Middle East War Zone ribbons are issued and the Pacific War Zone ribbon goes to 177,926 Seamen. If the numbers appear too high it is because most men qualify for two and sometimes three war zone ribbons.

The exact number of Seamen who are Prisoners of War is debatable. Captain Duffy sets the figure at 509 Seamen and 1 woman. Other sources go as high as 607 Seaman and 2 women. One of the reasons for the difference in figures is that some American Seamen who are captured are not sailing on American flagships.

As mentioned earlier 9,512 Seamen "passed over the bar". Most of these Seamen, along with their Navy Gunner shipmates, have only the waves for their tombstones.

A very revealing figure is the total number of Seamen who received the Combat Bar. A total of 114,145 Z-Men are eligible for the Combat Ribbon. No other service has that high a percentage of servicemen who serve in combat situations. The actual number of Combat Merchant Seamen would be much higher except for the requirements. A Seaman can be traveling in a convoy when enemy subs and planes attack. The ship on the portside and the ship on the starboard side are both hit and are sunk. This is real combat, but if the ship he is on is not hit and no one on board is injured, he does not qualify for the ribbon. Crazy, but that's the way the requirement reads.

The Merchant Marine Academy requires the Cadets to log sea time. The Cadets, of course, share the same dangers as the Seamen and Gunners. The academy has 123 killed. It is the only military academy to lose a student.

The Z-Man returns home. An interesting but dangerous part of his life is behind him. Whatever he is doing or intends to do just may be altered. For many there is a rude shock coming. Selective Service physical requirements are lowered and men who are 4-F are now 1-A. The Selective Service (Draft Board) now needs him. The 1-G classification means nothing now. Some of the Seamen are married, so the government does not call them, as there is no desire to pay extra for dependents. Some are now beyond the draft age, and some have disabilities that are beyond acceptance. Imagine that! They can stand an 8-hour watch 7 days a week plus extra work on a Merchant Ship but they are not good enough for a position on a Navy Ship. The rest? Uncle Sam Needs You. A few are smart enough to contact their congressmen who intervene for them and their I-G classification is honored. The rest of the Z-Men become soldiers, marines, sailors or airmen. The actual percentage of Z-Men who are called for further service will never be known. S.S. Samuel Parker Chapter American Merchant Marine and U.S.N. Armed Guard Chapter conducts a poll of its members. The result of the poll (admittedly a small sample) shows that exactly 62% of the Z-Men donned the uniform of another service. This is outrageous. They, again, answer their country's call. Not one seaman is reported to have run off to Canada to avoid the Draft.

To trace just a few of these Z-Men in their new service careers, consider the following: <u>Edward "Ed" Dierkes</u>---U.S. Army. Ed is a 16-year old Seaman who sees more seawater by the time he is of draft age (18) than most of the other branches veterans ever see. Al <u>"Bud" La Gates</u> ---U.S. Army. Bud is another 16-year old Seaman. He goes into Leyte on a Liberty Ship right after the invasion when he is still sixteen. Bud is wounded twice in Korea and receives two Purple Hearts   Frank Kodelja ---U.S. Army. Frank is 4-F (color blind) but like all other Seamen he volunteers for the U.S. Merchant Marine. After the war Frank is drafted into the U.S. Army where he serves for 30 years and retires as a full colonel. After Frank's retirement he works tirelessly for the Merchant Seaman veterans Although he serves 30 years in the Army and only 2½ years as a Z-Man, he always feels that the U.S. Merchant Seamen are treated unfairly. Frank's brother, Walter, served in the Naval Armed Guard. Frank sadly "crossed over the bar.."

One of the worst examples of injustice to a seaman is the way Mike Pappas of Lowell, Massachusetts, was treated. Mike, while serving in the Merchant Marine, thinks that he has to serve in the army also. He enters the army and completes basic training and is doing his time like all soldiers. Then a directive from the army comes down that releases former mariners to go back to sea. Mike thinks, "Okay, I'll get an Honorable Discharge from the army and ship out". This he does until the war ends. Mike goes home and then gets a letter from the Draft Board ordering him to report for army duty. No trouble, Mike thinks and he goes down to straighten out this little problem. He is informed that he is eligible for the draft, as he only served 11 months in the U.S. Army and everyone must serve 12 months. Mike goes back to sea. Who said life is fair?

MILITARY LEADERS COMMENTS

The thoughts of General Dwight Eisenhower and General Douglas MacArthur concerning the U.S. Merchant Marine have been aired. Other military leaders are also expressing their thoughts.

Admiral Ernest King "During the past three and a half years, the Navy has been dependent on the Merchant Marine to supply our far-flung fleet and bases. Without this support, the Navy could not have accomplished its mission. Consequently, it is fitting that the Merchant Marine share in our success as it shared in our trials."

Winston S. Churchill "The Battle of the Atlantic" was a dominating factor all through the war. Never for one moment could we forget that everything happening elsewhere on land, at sea, in the air, depended ultimately on its outcome.....Many gallant actions and incredible feats of endurance are recorded, but the deeds of those who perished will never be known. Our Merchant Seamen displayed their highest qualities and the brotherhood of the sea was never more strikingly shown than in their determination to defeat the U-Boat."

<u>Colonel Paul W. Tibbets, Pilot of the Enola Gay</u> "You guys put your a--- on the line everyday. Those of us old timers know and appreciate what you did."

<u>President George W. Bush</u> "......Today we honor the courage, determination, and service of our Nation's Merchant Mariners and remember the many who have given their lives in defense of our country. Their work reflects the patriotism and devotion to duty that makes America great......." (National Maritime Day Proclamation 2006).

<u>Marshal Georgi K.Zhukov</u> " We sincerely hold the memory of the killed British and American Seamen who despite the dangerous situation at sea, despite the fact that they faced death every mile of the way, supplied us (USSR) with some of the materials under the Lend Lease Agreement"

<u>Vice-Admiral Emery S. Land</u> "..I feel that the officers and men of the Merchant Marine, the operators serving as agents of our government, and the men and women of W.S.A.—all these citizens have served their country well. Any industry that can accomplish what this one has done in wartime can justify its great promise in peace."

<u>President Ronald Reagan's National Maritime Day Proclamation in 1988</u>
"The importance of the Merchant Marine to our national defense was never more clear than in World War II when, at a cost of more than 6,000 lives and a loss of 733 ships, the American Merchant Marine never faltered in delivering cargo for our Armed Forces throughout the world."

<u>Ernie Pyle</u> is not a military leader, but he is probably the best known WWII war correspondent and is truly loved by the fighting men with whom he dies in combat. "The crews of those big freighters were members of the Merchant Marine. The greatest apprehension I've found in the Anzio-Nettuno area is not among the men ashore-----but among the crews of ships that sit out in the Mediterranean, unloading---they are subject to shelling from land and air raids

from the sky. Their situation, I'll admit, is not an enviable one." A ship is assigned the name Ernie Pyle after he is killed.

Governor Ellis Arnall of Georgia in 1946 said, "We of America owe too much to these officers and men to forget them. We must not have short memories or permit others to forget. Certainly I think Merchant Seamen are entitled to these benefits. Government agencies and high officials have constantly paid tribute to these men for their deeds and devotion to duty. I think we have given enough lip service. We should have taken action long ago to give these men their just rights. This must not be token legislation—but something real, tangible and worthwhile." President Franklin C. Roosevelt "The (Mariners) have written one of its most brilliant chapters. They have delivered the goods when and where needed in every theater of operations and across every ocean in the biggest, the most difficult and most dangerous job ever taken." General Marshall—May 18, 1945 "America's Merchant Marine has carried out its war mission with great distinction, and has demonstrated its ability to meet the challenge of redeploying our full power to the Pacific." Admiral Nimitz May 18, 1945 "The United States Merchant Marine played an important part in the achievement of victory in Europe, and it is destined to play an even more important role in helping to finish off the Japanese. To move great quantities of war materials, principal sources of supply across 6,000 miles of ocean to battlefronts in the Far East is the formidable task now confronting our Merchant Fleet. We are confident it will be done quickly and efficiently in keeping with the high standards of accomplishment set by the Merchant Marine in every war in our history."

General Vandegrift May 18, 1945 "The men and ships of the Merchant Marine have participated in every landing operation by the United States Marine corps from Guadalcanal to Iwo Jima—and we know they will be at hand with supplies and equipment when American amphibious forces hit the beaches of Japan itself. On Maritime Day we of the Marine Corps salute the men of the Merchant Fleet."

Although not a U.S. Leader the words of our former enemy must be included. "Arguably, the best people to ask about who contributed the most would be a defeated enemy. For World War II, the German records indicate the greatest threat came not from forces on the ground or in the air but from the Merchant Marine. Because it took 7 to 15 tons of supplies to support a soldier for one year, without the Merchant Marine the liberating U.S., British and Canadian troops would fail"(Rexford St. Louis Post-Dispatch July 17, 2006).

As the Merchant Ships come back to the United States after the war is over the Seamen have to face reality. The expectations and hopes for the G I Bill and other veterans' benefits are not going to be a reality. The Z-Man does not sit down and feel sorry for himself. He proves that he is a resilient type at every invasion, on the Murmansk run, and facing Kamikazes. He takes his place in society like everyone else. Just maybe because he doesn't have the G I Bill, he works a little harder. If he wants to attend college, he doesn't have a free ride so he attends classes by day; at night he tends bar, works a night shift in a factory, or drives a taxi. If he applies for a job he doesn't have the extra points given for serving in the military that other veterans have, so he has to sell himself. Once he is employed he is there on an equal basis with everyone else. He knows that he will have to exercise a little more determination and effort to move up in the industrial world.

Does he succeed? Yes! Is he superior to others? Of course not. A study of this subject would be interesting, but in all probability Merchant Seamen are like all other veterans—a cross section of society. Turner Publishing Company in its 1993 U.S. Merchant Marine gives a nice review of ships and Z-Men in World War II and they have published a thumbnail sketch of where the Z-Man is in 1993 and what he is doing. This book devotes 59 pages to the U.S. Merchant Marine veterans. There are 639 Z-Men listed. Many have a photo of when they were a Seaman in WW II and a current picture. For those interested Turner publishing address is P.O. Box 3101, 412 Broadway, Paducah, Ky 42001.

A recently published book, <u>Maritime</u> has been produced by S.S. Stephen Hopkins Chapter of American Merchant Marine Veterans located in the Dallas-Fort Worth area. This Merchant Marine Veterans chapter is named after the Gallant Ship—S.S. Stephen Hopkins (p 90) and the man for whom the ship is named (p. 116). This book is a compilation of a number of tales of the sea by 52 former Z-Men. It was published for the Twentieth American Merchant Marine National Convention in May 24-28 in Texas. Both books are well worth procuring for anyone with an interest in World War II and the Merchant Marine.

Z-MEN FIGHT FOR VETERAN STATUS

The U.S. Merchant Marine Seamen are not happy with the treatment they receive following World War II. A conflict is to be waged. Not with cannons and machine guns but with logic, reasoning and determination. The Seamen want the recognition they so richly deserve. All the military leaders, <u>the men who were there</u>, have nothing but praise and admiration for the Z-Men. It is the politicians, the bureaucrats, the men who were not there, who have made the decisions. Now they must contend with some of the most zealous individuals they will ever meet —The Z-Men.

This is not a short confrontation. It will take the Z-Men 43 years to win this fight. Every one feels that President Franklin D. Roosevelt would have settled it in the 1940's. Without President Roosevelt to champion the cause the solution is much harder to obtain. In addition to the lackadaisical attitude of the politicians there is opposition from the other veteran groups, especially the V.F.W. (Veterans of Foreign Wars) who claim the Seamen got rich in World War II.

These Seamen are, in many cases, the young men who are just out of high school who go down to the recruiter office to join the Navy or the Coast Guard. The Navy or Coast Guard recruiters, if their quotas are filled, send them to the United States Maritime Service office. The comment most often heard is, "That's where your service is needed".

The United States Maritime Service recruits active and retired Seamen, Navy, and Coast Guardsmen for leadership and instruction. In as much as the USMS is an official U.S. Government organization these men, as well as the new recruits, believe then and still believe to this day that they are in a <u>uniformed armed service</u>. Instruction in cannon and modern gun training reinforced this belief. As soon as they embark on their first voyage, they are entering a hazardous war zone with the ever present possibility of air attacks, submarines firing torpedoes and floating or submerged mines. Does this appear to the young Seaman as a normal 8-5 job? No, this is a Service!

Prior to completion of his Maritime Service training and being assigned his first ship, he may hear President Roosevelt's December 13th speech in 1942. President Franklin D. Roosevelt sends his personal greetings to the Sheepshead Bay Training station in Brooklyn, N.Y. He says, "It is with a feeling of great pride that I send my heartiest congratulations and best wishes to the officers and men of the new U.S. Maritime Training Station at Sheepshead Bay, New York. Ten thousand apprentice Seamen in training at one station is a magnificent achievement, and the entire country joins me in wishing you every success and in paying tribute to you men of the Merchant Marine who are so gallantly working and fighting side by side with our Army and Navy to defend the way of life which is so dear to us all "(U.S.Maritime Service: The Forgotten Service http://www. Usmm.org/usms.html). Seamen would like to know how fighting is not part of a military service. Captain H.H. Dreany, Assistant Commandant, U.S.M.S. stated, "United States Maritime Service was a government service, and graduates were representatives of the United States government "(U.S.Maritime Service: The Forgotten service http://www.Usmm.org/usms.html).

In 1944 when President Franklin Roosevelt signed the G I Bill of Rights, he states, "I trust Congress will soon provide similar opportunities to members of the Merchant Marine who have risked their lives time and time again during the war for the welfare of their country."

Seamen are not without humor. Some unknown Seaman artist draws a black and white picture of crewmembers in a lifeboat. Some other unknown Seaman sarcastically adds the words, "Will the V.F.W. accept us?" (See photo p 158 p).

The years drag on and still the Seaman does not have veteran status. In 1977 Senator Barry Goldwater, an Air Force Reserve General, sponsors a bill to grant veteran status to the W.A.S.P. s (Womens Air force Service Pilots). Most Seamen are probably not opposed to women being granted veteran status. They do argue that Seamen, who have been involved in actual combat in a war zone, should become veterans as well as some individuals who flew an airplane in the

Will the VFW Accept Us?

LIFEBOAT

158p

States. Congress insists on set procedures for any group to apply for status. The U.S. Defense Secretary designates the Air Force Secretary to administer a Civilian/Military Service Review Board. The W.A.S.P.s become the first group to be awarded veteran status and the legal criteria are set. Now the Merchant Seamen will surely receive veteran status? NO! This Civilian/Military Service Review Board will reject the U.S. Merchant Marine applications for veteran status from 1977 to 1987. In World War II there was a poster of a rugged looking seaman with a sea bag over his shoulder with the words," You bet I am going back to sea." Now this poster is reproduced with the words changed to "You bet I am a combat veteran". (See photo p 159 q)

One of the jokes making the rounds among former Seamen is a child asks his grandfather what he did in the war. The old WWII Seaman tells his grandson, "Nothing, at least according to the federal government." The joke has gone on long enough. In 1987 Former P.O.W.'s Stanley Willner, (p 115-116) Edward Fitzgerald, and Dennis Roland, (115-116) who have repeatedly had their applications rejected decide something has to be done. Knowing that their applications meet all the necessary qualifications they decide to sue in The Federal Court. Taking the U.S. Air Force Secretary, Edward C. Aldridge Jr., to court results in a ruling that the Secretary has "abused its discretion...applied unstated and vague criteria ....frustrated.....purpose of implementing regulations" (Chronology of U.S. Merchant Marine Struggle for Recognition and Justice

"YOU BET I AM A COMBAT VETERAN!"

U.S. MERCHANT MARINE

http://www.USMM.org 2/22/05). Unfortunately Roland had "crossed the Bar." His replacement was Merchant Seaman Veteran Lane Kirkland, head of the A.F.L-C.I.O.

It takes over 43 years, but now the Z-Man is a veteran. He has fulfilled that part of the poster (p 160 r) that reads "AT LEAST SOME DAY---" Are the Seamen happy? The ones still alive are, of course. How about the thousands who have already 'crossed over the bar'? For them it is too late. For the widows and children there is some satisfaction.

Now that the Z-Men are officially veterans a number of new rules and regulations requiring legislation are enacted. The Merchant Marine veterans' organizations are recognized. The other veterans' organizations, such as the American Legion, invite the mariners to become members. Many already are members but now they can list Merchant Marine along with the other branches in which they served. The one exception to this change is the V.F.W.; as individuals they are not recognized at the national level. The policy set by the national level is that the Merchant Marine is not a service and cannot be recognized. as one. Local levels continue to accept Z-Men.

The Seaman with veteran status is entitled to the use of the veterans' hospital and can receive medical care. If necessary he resides in a Veterans' Home. Of great importance is he will have a U. S. flag on his coffin, and if he desires he may be buried in a National Cemetery under a Veteran's marker. The

I WAS THAT WHICH OTHERS DID NOT

WANT TO BE
I WENT WHERE OTHERS FEARED TO GO
AND DID WHAT OTHERS FAILED TO DO.
I HAVE SEEN THE FACE OF TERROR,
FELT THE STINGING COLD OF FEAR.
I HAVE CRIED, PAINED, AND HOPED..
BUT MOST OF ALL

I HAVE LIVED TIMES OTHERS WOULD
SAY
WERE BEST FORGOTTEN.

AT LEAST SOMEDAY I WILL BE ABLE TO
SAY

THAT I WAS PROUD OF WHAT I WAS
...A SEAMAN

major benefits of the G I Bill have long passed the Z-Man by. He is not attending college or a trade school and by now he has paid off his home. He does receive that Honorable Discharge. Its is a United States Coast Guard discharge, but it has an American Merchant Marine statement. (See p 161 s)

The Secretary of the Air Force set August 15, 1945 as the end of the war for the U.S. Merchant Marine. Only mariners who sail in "ocean-going waters' before August 15, 1945 are given veteran status. It should be noted that no other service has any restriction. Z-Men who meet this requirement receive their honorable discharges along with a DD 214 Form sighting all citations and awards received. Now, these 50 year-old plus seamen have a Certificate of Discharge to hang on the wall quite possibly along side one that his son has earned. Many Seamen already have a Certificates of Discharge for serving in another service after WWII.

The Seamen are happy for this victory, but it does not go far enough.. The date of August 15, 1945 is the cutoff date. This is not fair. President Harry S. Truman declares in Proclamation 2714 that December 31, 1946 is the official end of hostilities for WW II. Congress follows by making this date into law. This is the date the V.A. (Veterans Administration) recognizes for all services. All services----
--except The Merchant Marine.

August 15, 1945 was the date of Japan accepting defeat, but the official documents were not signed until September 2, 1945 on the Battleship Missouri.

Honorable Discharge

from the Armed Forces of the United States of America

This is to certify that

GEORGE ELLWOOD WARD JR

was Honorably Discharged from the

United States Coast Guard

on the 15 day of AUGUST 1945

as a testimonial of Honest and Faithful Service

This certificate is awarded

Frederic J. Grady

Captain, U.S. Coast Guard

Issued pursuant to P.L. 95-202 for service in the 'American Merchant Marine in Oceangoing Service during the Period of Armed Conflict, December 7, 1941, to August 15, 1945.'

DD FORM 256 CG (REV. 5-60)

The U.S. Maritime trainee who does not get on a ship until August 16th or later is out of luck. Now a new conflict starts. The date of August 15, 1945 applies only to the Merchant Seamen and not to any other service. During the period in question August 16, 1945 to December 31, 1945 the United States has eleven ships sunk by mines. Of these eleven ships eight are Liberties. This does not include ships that sink because of storms or by running aground. As a result of these 11 ships going down after hitting mines, 10 Seamen are killed and 35 are wounded.

One of the leaders in this fight to get the Merchant Marine equal to all the other services in using December 31, 1946 as the end of WWII is Burt Young. Ex-Seaman Young is the author of <u>Should Veteran Status Be Dependent on a Kangaroo Court</u>? This book is probably the best and most complete source of information on this injustice. This history of a fight to right a wrong includes the name, dates, letters, and etc. of those individuals who are a party to this controversy. Burt Young is to be complimented for all the time and effort expended in this noble effort to correct this injustice. The patience and frustration that Young endured is beyond belief. Example: Seaman Young ".....I had submitted my application two years before Congress gave us veteran status. WHY DID SECRETARY JOHNSON KEEP MY APPLICATION OVER TWO YEARS BEFORE ACTING ON IT?" (Young <u>Should Veterans Status Be Dependent on a Kangaroo Court</u>? 2003)

In 1992 the Secretary of Transportation issues Veteran status to the U.S. Merchant Marine Academy Cadets who are killed in World War II. The same year the U.S. Air Force grants veteran status to W.A.S.P.s who had "washed out" of training. Some Seamen are still not recognized for the period from August 15, 1945 to December 31, 1946.

Finally in 1998 on Veterans' Day the President signs a bill into law granting veteran status for the mariners who served from August 15, 1945 to December 31, 1946. At last, after a 52-year wait, these men become veterans. Wait—one more thing. They are not given like any other veteran's discharge. There is a $30.00 fee! This is unbelievable; the government wants $30.00 for this piece of paper. This is the certificate that proclaims the seaman is honorably discharged. Again many do not live long enough to witness this. This leaves the question of veteran status for the Seamen during the Korean, Viet Nam, Desert Storm and Iraqi conflicts.

What does the Merchant Seamen <u>VETERAN</u> now do? He continues life as usual. There is a noticeable increase in interest in most veteran organizations including the American Merchant Marine Veterans, which has over 70 Merchant Marine chapters throughout the United States. Now that veteran status has been obtained there is much for these chapters to do. The S.S. Samuel Parker Chapter American Merchant Marine and Navy Armed Guard, located in St. Louis, Mo., is a good example of what most chapters are doing. After receiving veteran status the first really big project is to place a monument dedicated to The Merchant Marine and to all those who made the supreme sacrifice in a prominent location. Funds are raised, a monument is designed, and a location is approved. Every thing moves along smoothly and permission is received to put the monument in Jefferson Barracks National Cemetery. A large appropriate monument is designed and, of course, the outline of a Liberty Ship is included on it. It is thought that this is the first Merchant Marine monument in a National cemetery. Now a snag is encountered. All national cemeteries are under the administration of the V.A. (Veterans Administration) and new regulations are now in effect. The large monument does not meet the proper specifications and must be redesigned. The new design of the monument with the new specifications is presented and approved. The monument is dedicated with a large number of state and local officials present. A U.S. Representative gave the dedication speech to a very large crowd. This smaller monument is located in an area designed just for this purpose. In retrospect, while the Seamen Veterans would have liked the larger monument in the other area, this area is more appropriate. The monument is placed in line with all the others and all are the same size. Here with monuments representing the U.S. Marine Corps, U.S. Submarines, U.S. Navy and Coast Guard, Destroyer Escorts and A.P.D. Third Infantry Division, Fourth Marine Division, and All Sea Service Women---Yeomen F. Waves, Navy Women, Navy Nurses, SPARS, and Women Marines, this monument is equal to all the others.

It is next to the All Sea Service Women Monument, and this also is appropriate. (See photos p 165 t)

Next comes an anchor monument project. This is quite an ambitious goal. Where do you find an anchor in St. Louis 700 plus miles from the nearest sea? With the assistance of President Mike Sacco of the S.I.U. (Seafarers International Union), an 18,000 lb. (9 ton) anchor is located and is available. It's not off a Liberty. Actually it was previously on the U.S.S. Langley, an aircraft carrier that earned nine battle stars. The seamen are delighted with it. One little problem does arise. How does the anchor get from Florida to St. Louis? Again assistance is forth coming. Noel Stasiak, a C.P.O. in the Navy, works for a trucking company. Pulling some strings Stasiak gets the anchor delivered to St. Louis. Now that it is here, where is it to be located? Fortunately Mr. Ralph Weichert Superintendent of Soldiers' Memorial, located in downtown St. Louis, gives permission to place the monument on the grounds of the Soldiers' Memorial. It is the best possible location in the State of Missouri and is a striking view. One of the large construction companies, (Budrovich), in St. Louis volunteers to set the anchor in place. This is not an easy task, as a very solid concrete base must be laid, and this very heavy anchor must be lifted over sidewalks and up steps. The St. Louis city engineers assist in the installation of the anchor. With the cooperation of the Navy League, the anchor is dedicated to all seafarers i.e.

JEFFERSON BARRACKS MONUMENT

165 t

Marine, Coast Guard, Merchant Marine, and Navy. Later an appropriate anchor chain is added. (See photo p166u)

S.S. Samuel Parker Chapter meets 10 times a year at the S.I.U. (Seafarers International Union) hall courtesy of President Mike Sacco S.I.U. Ms Becky Sleeper is the St. Louis Port Agent (S.I.U.) and is a seafarer and member of S.S. Samuel Parker Chapter.

The S.S. Samuel Parker Seamen engage in wreath laying ceremonies and represent the U.S. Merchant Marine in parades. Representation, in cooperation with the other services, is made at the Armed Forces Memorials, where all six services--Army, Navy, Air Force, Coast Guard, Merchant Marine, and Marines have plaques and flags displayed. There is complete cooperation among all Service veterans and there is no animosity. One thing that the Seamen are working on is the presentation of the Merchant Marine anthem in concerts. At many concerts the anthems of all the services are played in tribute to our servicemen. The Merchant Marine anthem is sometimes omitted and any Seaman present talks to the band director following the concert. He requests that they include it with their medley and offers to provide the music for it. The band directors are always willing to comply. This song is now presented on both local and national concerts programs (See p. 166 v & w).

The name S.S. Samuel Parker was selected for the chapter in honor of the Liberty Ship of that name that was the first Gallant Ship so honored (p.90-91).

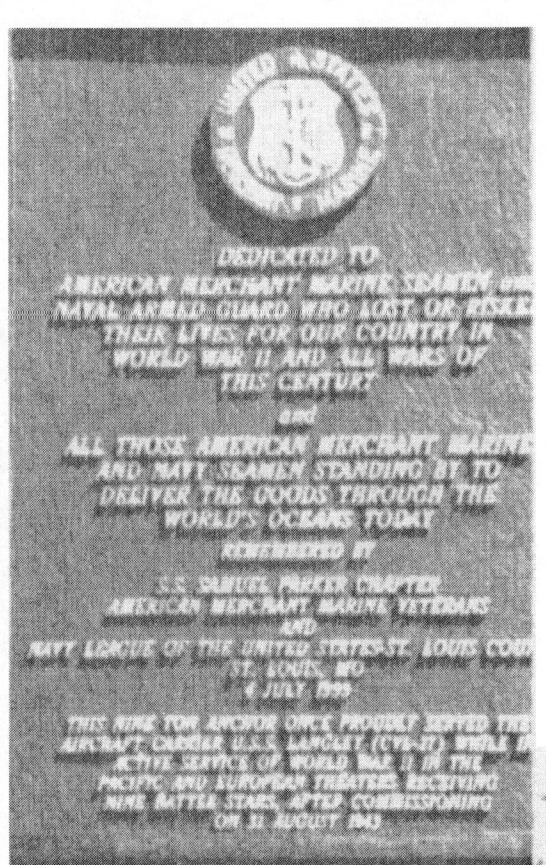

ANCHOR AT SOLDIER'S MEMORIAL

MERCHANT MARINE ANTHEM

CHORUS
HEAVE HO! — MY LADS, HEAVE HO! — It's a long, long way to
go, — It's a long, long pull with our hat-ches full, Bra-ving the
wind, bra-ving the sea, Fight-ing the treach-er-ous foe, HEAVE HO! — MY
LADS, HEAVE HO! — Let the sea roll high or low, —
— We can cross an-y o-cean, sail an-y ri-ver, give us the
goods and we'll de-liv-er, Damn the sub-ma-rine! — We're the
men of the Mer-chant Ma-rine! HEAVE -rine! —

The S.S. Samuel Parker sustained 250 holes from one attack. Other chapters are named after ships, Seamen, or geographic locations. (See p. 167 x)

Becky Sleeper, as mentioned before (p 166), is a member of S.S. Samuel Parker. She is not an honorary member, but is a regular member. She earned that right by sailing on a U.S. Merchant Ship in Desert Storm. As St. Louis Port Agent she assists individuals in providing information on the U.S. Merchant Marine and on the benefits of going to sea. If a person desires to go to sea, Becky will walk the individual through the paper work, the physical examination, etc. and will set up enrollment at the S.I.U. Piney Point Training Center.

Becky and others females sailing today have made it necessary to think before saying "seaman". If it is a man, he is a seaman and this term is okay. Referring to a group as seamen is no longer in vogue as there are women sailing. While mariner is the preferred title, sailors or seafarer is acceptable. Never use the term Merchant Marines!

The Merchant Marine is no longer the forgotten service. In reality, the only location that forgot the Merchant Marine was Washington D.C. The Seamen knew they were in the service when Seamen were court-marshaled. Civilians are tried as civilians in criminal or civil courts, and the military tries service personnel in a court-marshal. They knew they were in the service because General Douglas MacArthur said they were. They knew they were in the service when President Franklin D. Roosevelt said, "you men of the Merchant Marine who are so

Bomb Rips Vessel With 250 Holes—
BUT OH, BUOY, IT FLOATS!

The Liberty Ship Samuel Parker, still showing some of the 250 holes caused by one 1,000-pound bomb hit, is pictured back home after weathering 50 enemy air attacks during the invasion of Sicily. (AP Wirephoto.)

S.S. SAMUEL PARKER

gallantly working and fighting side by side with our Army and Navy to defend the way of life which is so dear to us all" (U.S. Maritime Service; the Forgotten Service—http://www.usmm.org/usms.html). They knew they were in the service at every invasion. They knew they were in the service when submarines attacked their ships. They knew they were in the service when aircraft attacked them

They knew they were in the service when the Director in charge of Selective Service, General Lewis B. Hershey wrote,"Service in the Merchant Marine, considering its importance to the war effort and the hazards involved, is so closely allied to the service in the armed forces that men found by the local board to be actively engaged at sea may well be considered as engaged in active defense of the country. Such service may properly be considered as tantamount to military service (U.S. Merchant Marine Turner Publisher 1993 p 27).

It appears that some foreign countries think more of the U.S. Merchant Marine than our politicians in Washington D.C. do. As a commemoration of the war years, Russia has a special Russian Medal for the Seamen and Gunners who made the Murmansk run (See Chart p 168 y). To further show their appreciation they have a commemoration medal for anyone who served on a Merchant Marine ship any where in the world. (Remember what Marshal Georgi Zhukov said p.154). China authorized a medal for any one spending 30 days or more in the Pacific War Zone.

U.S. MERCHANT MARINE
MEDALS AND DECORATIONS
To you who answered the call of your country and served in its Merchant Marine . . . President Harry S. Truman
DEPARTMENT OF DEFENSE AND FOREIGN GOVERNMENTS RECOGNITION

WORLD WAR II COMMEMORATIVE MEDALS

COM-014.2
China World War II

WWII China
War Memorial

Soviet Commemorative Medal

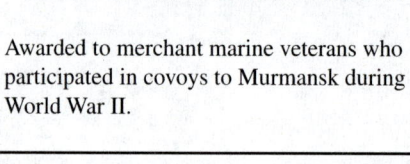

Awarded to merchant marine veterans who participated in covoys to Murmansk during World War II.

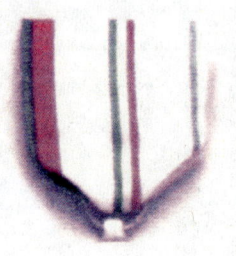

COM-018.2
China · Burma · India

Soviet Commemorative
All Allied Forces
Any Where

COM-035.2
Merchant Marine
World War II

COM-036.2
Armed Guard
World War II

169 z

Yugoslavia, now split into a number of countries, had a medal for any one sailing in any War Zone. There is commemorative medal for those in the C.B.I. (China, Burma, India) War Zone. The United States honors those men sailing on Merchant Ships with a commemorative medal. This is a medal with either a Merchant Marine Bar or an Armed Guard Bar (See photo p 169 z).

The Seamen, as all veterans, are happy the war is over. After the second A-Bomb is dropped the Japanese are threatened with a third A-Bomb. They decide that they have had enough. The U.S.A. pulls off a bluff that saves an untold number of lives. There is no third bomb. Many years later there are those who criticized President Harry Truman for authorizing the use of these bombs. The men in the service tell those individuals in a hurry that they are dead wrong. The loss of men in the invasions of the islands, especially Tarawa, indicates the extreme conditions they would have faced in attacking Japan on its home territory where they would really dig in. They would have been fighting everyone— including women and children.

Estimates of the carnage runs as high as 2,500.000 casualties for the Japanese and over 1,000,000 for the Americans and the Allies. Not only are the forces in the Pacific Theater happy, but the troops that had just defeated the Axis know that they have been given a break and know that they won't have to go there. As one Battle of the Bulge veteran, Vernon Kruse, said, "If I see Harry Truman in the hereafter, I'm sure going to shake his hand". Up to this point the Japanese military would not even consider giving up. Some

Japanese historians say that some of the civilian leaders wanted to surrender, all to no avail. This terrible bomb gives the peace element an opportunity to argue for peace. An Emperor Hirohito advisor said the A-Bomb aided the peace movement and called this "a golden opportunity given by heaven for Japan to end the war."

ARTIFICAL FISH REEFS

The Liberties have been languishing for years in the reserve fleet. The number has been diminishing as the ships make those final trips to the ship breakers. Some fall in the category of the Chase Project. Very simply they would <u>C</u>ut <u>H</u>oles <u>A</u>nd <u>S</u>ink 'Em in deep water. Realizing that a better use of these ships is available, Congress passed the Artificial Fish Reef Program in 1972. Some of the Liberties are given to the states that can use them for fish reefs. Some states will be able to greatly increase the fish and other sea life in their areas with these old Liberties.

Selected Liberties are sunk in various locations to form artificial fish reefs. It is a known fact that odd objects, such as truck and automobile tires, worn out items like refrigerators and stoves, wrecked motor vehicles, etc. lying at the bottom of the ocean serve a purpose. These objects attract smaller fish and shellfish as a hiding place and a place for them to hide their eggs. Sea vegetation will flourish in these areas. In areas where there are few rock formations there are few fish. This is the situation in California and in the South Atlantic and Gulf regions in the U.S.A. The states of Virginia, North Carolina, and Georgia on the

Southern Atlantic Coast, and the Gulf states of Florida, Alabama, Mississippi, and Texas can use these artificial fish reefs. Forty-one Liberties are selected for this purpose in these two areas. One more will serve the same purpose in California.

The Liberties are prepared for the sinkings. All machinery is taken off. All masts and deck obstructions are removed to prevent passing ships from suffering damages. All oil and lubricants are cleaned off the ships. Holes are cut in the sides of the ships to allow sea life to move freely in and out. The Liberties take their last trips and they are sunk in the selected locations.

These ships will still be useful well into the 21st Century. Can anyone imagine what Kaiser and the other shipbuilders, if they were alive today, would say if they heard about this. Knowing Kaiser, instead of bemoaning the fact that the Liberties are being sunk, he would propose a new fish reef ship constructed with the enhancement of fishing as a goal.

The mustard gas explosion detailed in chapter four is not the only poison gas episode in and after WWII. The S.S. Le Baron Russell Briggs is scuttled on August 18, 1970 on the Chase Program over 250 miles from Florida. Prior to the sinking, lethal nerve gas is found leaking from cases that are corroded. The 67 tons of gas hydrolyzes under the tremendous pressure deep in water rendering it harmless.

Following World War II The Baltic Sea becomes a dumping ground for chemical bombs. A total of 46,000 tons is disposed of in this area. Then between

1945 and 1949 the British dump 127,000 tons of chemical and conventional weapons in the Norwegian Trench.

Now in the 21st century the problem of poison gas continues to exist. As the containers continue to corrode their gases escape. The gases become solid as they mix with seawater. Many fishermen are injured when their fishing gear comes in contact with these substances.

Both the U.S. and the Allies and the enemy have poison gas in various forms in WWII. Does neither side use it because they know that the other side also has it? Does Adolph Hitler, who is gassed in WWI, refrain from using it because of that experience (Reminick Nightmare In Bari p225)? Whatever the reason the poison gas is not used, thank God!

The U.S. Merchant Marine Academy, located in King's Point, New York, has a couple of firsts during and after World II. It was the first and only U.S. Service Academy to have cadets in action. It was the first service to academically accept women cadets (Allsup "We deliver the goods" December 2005). World War II cadets receive veteran status in 1992.

LAST OF THE LIBERTIES

There is an old story of a Z-Man planning to retire from the sea. He says he is going to put an oar over his shoulder and start walking inland. He says he will walk until someone asks him what is that on his shoulder. He says he will stick the oar in the ground and that is where he will retire. Z-Men didn't carry oars on their shoulders, but many returning to civilian life do not live in coastal towns. A Z-Man, who is not privy to San Francisco newspapers, is surprised to hear that there is one "Last Liberty Ship" still in existence. In 1980 this ship is refurbished at Pier 3, Fort Mason, San Francisco, as a memorial to all those who fought at sea in World War II. It is built between May and June 1943 at the New England Shipbuilding Company in South Portland, Maine(McCombs <u>World War II Strange and Fascinating Facts</u> 1983 p. 288).

<u>THE FINAL TWO LIBERTIES</u>

The S.S. Jeremiah O'Brien has a short, but colorful wartime history—two and one half years. At the Normandy Invasion she makes eleven landings. From New Orleans she carries 10,000 tons of bombs through the Panama Canal and delivers them to New Guinea. She travels to Chile, Peru, India, China, Australia, and the Philippines. On her last trip the war ends and after 39,439,700 revolutions of the propeller she arrives back in San Francisco, California. In addition to a full cargo she brings to the States nine war brides (Navy) and three children (Jaffee <u>The Last Liberty</u> p 286). After two and one half years in the Atlantic, the Pacific, and the Indian Oceans, she is placed in the Reserve Fleet at Anchorage 26, Suisun Bay. (San Francisco, California). Suisun Bay is just one of eight Reserve Fleets. These ships are ready for a national emergency and are preserved with a thick coat of cosmoline. The preservative grease cosmoline, hardens into a thick protective film as a protection against rust.

The years go by and the Liberties are dropped from military plans. They are just too slow and too old. They have outlived their usefulness. After 1963 the Liberties are pulled out of the fleet and are sold or scrapped. There the O'Brien sits with portholes and doors open. Birds find a good place to nest. Paint is pealing off and she is getting rusty.

The Maritime Commission is surveying some 800 Liberties and rating them from best to worst. Some are sold and the rest are scrapped. The O'Brien is found to be in the best shape of all the Liberties in Suisun Bay. The O'Brien has only been used for what she was designed. She has never been altered. All furniture and equipment is in place and has not been marked up or abused. Other than the fact that the guns are removed, she is in her original shape. The war charts, instructions, even the Captain's books from the Normandy Invasion are all located in drawers.

Realizing what a gem she is, Admiral Thomas J. Patterson keeps moving the O'Brien down the scrap list. She is moved to prevent the scrap dealers from seeing her. They prevent her from being raided by the Navy, and they protect her from vandals. Finally she is the only Liberty left and some action has to be taken. Some funds are made available providing matching funds, materials and labor could be obtained from private sources. Funds and volunteers make this project a reality.

The O'Brien is moving to Bethlehem Shipyard. Tugs are employed to move her when it is decided to sail her down, if possible. This is the first attempt to get steam up on a ship that has been dead for thirty-four years. The O'Brien does get steam up and travels the 40 miles without tugs. The Seafaring Unions pitch in for the refurbishing of the ship. When they finish she looks like she is brand new. The N.M.U., Boilermakers Local No 6, S.U.P., S.I.U., and M.E.B.A. put in a total of 1,145 hours to accomplish this feat (Jaffee The Last Liberty p 314).

The S.S. Jeremiah O'Brien is next moved to Fort Mason to be opened to the public daily. Memorial Cruises are conducted around the San Francisco Bay at certain times of the year. One former crewmember who regularly sees another shipmate said, "Why don't we take our wives and take a cruise?" To which the other old seaman replied, "Are you nuts? We got paid $87.50 a month to sail her and you want to pay $75.00 per person for a one-day cruise." Both old Z-Men pay visits to the old Liberty. A souvenir program containing photos and the project history is presented to those taking a cruise on the old WWII Liberty (S.S. Jeremiah O'Brien 1985).

The S.S. Jeremiah O'Brien is about to undertake a long trip across the Atlantic Ocean in 1994. Can a ship built to last five years weather the North Atlantic? The O'Brien is attempting to go through the Panama Canal and over to France to participate in the 50th anniversary of D Day ceremony. She stops in

England and then moves on to Cherbourg, France and arrives there on June 23, 1994. "At Normandy, where 50 years ago 5,500 ships eclipsed the horizon, she was the sole survivor of the original armada. The President of the United States, who was not yet born when she was built, was piped aboard. The 20,000- mile trek from the Golden Gate to Normandy and home again may well be the Jeremiah O'Brien's longest and last voyage"(Last of the Liberty Ships http://www.cascobay.com/history/libship/libship.htm). Several other WWII ships break down on the way to the ceremony so they are unable to participate in the Normandy celebration.

The response the O'Brien receives is overwhelming. There are parades, fireworks, and bands. There are three and four masted schooners, square-riggers, tall ships. and warships with the high level of excitement continuing everywhere they go. There are ships from Chile, Norway, the Ukraine, South Africa, Brazil, Denmark, Italy, Ireland, Russia, as well as other countries. The list of ships goes on and on. "There will never be a gathering of ships like this again," said Captain Jahn (Jaffee S.S. Jeremiah O'Brien p 330). On July 14, Bastille Day, the WWII veteran Z-Men march in the parade and receive the greatest applause.

On her voyage home the O'Brien pays what is probably the last visit she will ever make to Portland, Maine, where she was born. She is the last unaltered Liberty that was "built by the mile and chopped off by the yard". It is there, in 1775, that Jeremiah O'Brien leads a group of patriots armed only with a few shot guns, some axes, and thirty pitchforks, captures the British man-of-war Margaretta in the first naval engagement of the War for Independence "(Jaffee S.S. Jeremiah O'Brien p 339). Thousands of people come out to see the O'Brien. Many in the crowd had worked in the Portland, Maine shipyards.

Five and a half months later the Jeremiah O'Brien is back home. She is given a hero's welcome, which she never received in WWII. Now she is berthed on the Embarcadero at Pier 45 in San Francisco. She cruises the third weekend of each month (See photo 177 aa). She is open to the public every day the rest of the month. An hour or two inspecting this grand old ship is time well spent. A real glimpse into the WW II Z-Man's life is waiting for you.

When the S.S. Jeremiah O'Brien is brought out of mothballs and made shipshape, she is thought to be the only Liberty left. Then in 1988 the S.S. John W. Brown is rededicated on Labor Day on the East Coast in Baltimore, Md.

The Brown is named after Canadian born John W. Brown. Brown is a patriot who spent most of his life building the Industrial Union of Maine Shipbuilding Workers of America. The S.S. John W. Brown is completed on September 7, 1942 and her first trip carries cargo to the Persian Gulf. She picks up a cargo of bauxite in South America on her way home. This first trip is her last, as a cargo ship. She becomes the first Liberty to be converted to a Troop Transport. As a troop carrier she makes nine trips during the war and four more following D Day. She transports Royal Navy officers and sailors when their

177 aa

ship had been torpedoed and she carried P.O.W. s. She carries many Allied troops (up to 1,000 at a time). Although she is never hit by enemy fire she sees plenty of action. Two Liberties near her are torpedoed and she suffers several minor collisions while earning two battle stars.

"This ship can carry almost 9,000 tons of cargo, about the same as 300 railroad box cars. Liberty Ships carry every conceivable cargo during the war—from beans to bullets. Some, like the John W. Brown, are also fitted out to carry troops as well as cargo "(Project Liberty Ship http://www.liberty-ship.com/html/brown/ss_john_w_brown.html).

Her wartime and postwar duties completed, the Brown is put on loan to New York City. She becomes a part of the Maritime Department of the Metropolitan Vocational High School. Students are taught all phases of seamanship. In 1982 the New York Board of Education returns the Brown to the U.S. Government. Four years earlier a group is formed to preserve the ship if and when the New York School system no longer needs or wants her. The preservation group moves her to Baltimore and she is rededicated on Labor Day 1988 and now cruises on Chesapeake Bay (See photo 178 bb). For anyone interested, the United States now has two Liberty Ships---The S.S. Jeremiah O'Brien on the West Coast and The S.S. John W. Brown on the East coast. The "Ugly Ducklings" are still alive!

S.S. JOHN BROWN

THE U.S. MERCHANT MARINE IN THE 21ST CENTURY

The Z-Men of World War II are forgotten for a long time and many have "crossed over the bar" before proper recognition for them is received. The S.I.U. is one of the strongest allies the Z-Men have in this struggle to obtain status. The S.I.U. has never wavered in its support for a strong U.S. Merchant Marine right up to the present. S.I.U. President Michael Sacco works tirelessly for the Seamen—both old and new. His remarks at the anchor dedication July 5, 1999 echo these thoughts with such comments as "It's important to establish the connection between today's active mariners and those who went before them. In fact, we who are in the S.I.U., make it a point to educate all of our new members about their maritime heritage—and the fact that they may be called upon as the nation's fourth arm of defense (Sacco—Remarks July 5, 1999).

The head of the U.S. Transportation Command (TRANSCOM) General Norton Schwartz and the outgoing commander of the U.S. Military Sealift Command (MSC) emphatically and enthusiastically credit the U.S. Merchant Marine for its ongoing role in Operation Enduring Freedom and Iraqi Freedom. General Schwartz said that S.I.U. President Michael Sacco is someone "who has excelled as a partner in matters of national defense with us" ("S.I.U We Could Not Have Fought This War Without You" http: // www.Seafarersrg/printFriendly.xml?thisContent=/log/2006/042006/mtdoif.xml). Vice Admiral Brewer said, "We could not have fought this war without this industry." These and other statements by high-ranking military leaders are indicative of their opinions about the seafarers the S.I.U. is turning out today.

Turning out today? That's right. The S.I.U. is turning out the seafarers today. The S.I.U. assumes the role that the W.S.A. performed in WW II. The United Maritime Authority was dissolved on March 2, 1946 and, of course, the U.S. Maritime Service discontinues training future seafarers at their three camps.

The school, Paul Hall Center for Maritime Training and Education, is located at Piney Point, Maryland and is funded by the S.I.U. and its contracted employers. This center goes far beyond the U.S. Maritime Service Training young men received in WW II. The Paul Hall Center continues the following disciplines

    Seafarers Harry Lundeberg School of Seamanship

    Joseph Sacco Fire Fighting and Safety School

    Thomas Browley, Sr., Education Center

    Bob McMillan Simulator Center

    Chesapeake Culinary Institute

    Paul Hall Library and Maritime Museum

The center is not just a training place for men and women beginning a sea career, but it is also for the mariners with some sea experience who want to acquire higher ratings. College program studies in nautical science technology (deck department students) or marine engineering technology (engine department students) can lead to an A.A.S. Degree (Associate of Applied Science) (Paul Hall Center for Maritime Training and Education p 70).

These mariners and officers graduating from the U.S. Merchant Marine Academy at Kings Point, N. Y. give the U. S. the best Seamen in the world.

Anyone interested can write or call for a catalog and information to:

Paul Hall Center for Maritime Training and Education

P.O. Box 75, Route 249

Piney Point, Md. 20674-0075   (301) 994-0010

On the Internet some information can be obtained at www.seafarers.org. Do not apply if you cannot pass a drug screening or are on a court ordered probation or parole.

Following the war many ships are laid up or sold. Their use in wartime was invaluable, but these ships are not the type of ships needed for the future. Did the United States go too far in reducing the Merchant Fleet? Yes. Moving cargo in and out of the United States by foreign ships has fallen into the category of "out sourcing". During Desert Storm some captains on foreign ships hauling desperately needed cargo by our troops are reported to be reluctant to put their ships in harm's way. This is again a wake- up call.

At the present time it appears that there will be more U.S. Ships in the Future. S.I.U. Present Sacco in his President's report wrote, " Captain Robert Johnston, vice president of S.I.U. -contracted Overseas Shipholding Groups

(OSG) announced that his company is strongly looking into investing in 17 new U.S. flag ships that would sail in the Jones Act trades. OSG is already scheduled to operate 10 new ships—the tankers being built at Aker Philadelphia Shipyard" (Sacco seafarers log April 2006). In the Seafarers Log it is reported that Horizon Lines announced March 17, 2006 an agreement in principle to charter 5 new U.S. flagships for 12-year terms from Ship Finance International Limited.

SEA STORIES

No history of Merchant Seamen would be complete without a few sea stories. Normally sea stories are enlarged on or embellished. In as much as this is an historical study of the U.S. Merchant Marine, the Liberty Ship and the Z-Men only true stories are related. Several do not include names, but are factual. The names have been deleted to protect the guilty. Two jokes are included.

Broke and Gutsy (Nutsy might be a better word). The Liberty pulls into Glasgow, Scotland and the crew goes on shore leave. One young seaman, who has had a little too much to drink, runs short of money. He decides he needs another beer or two, so he tries to borrow a few pounds (British money). Most everyone is still ashore. Those back on the ship are also broke. This young lad decides to ask for a draw (advance on pay) but the purser (finance officer) is ashore. Not very smart he goes up to the Captain's stateroom and knocks. No one answers, so he enters the room and shakes the Captain awake and asks for a draw. The answer he receives is not printable here. Hastily leaving the Captain, this young lad goes looking for a benefactor to no avail. Then he gets a bright (make that stupid) idea. He goes back to the Captain's room enters, shakes the captain awake again and asks, " If you won't give me a draw, will you loan me a little cash?" The young seaman does not think the Captain (who is a big man) can move that fast. It is pretty obvious that he is not going to get a loan. He now realizes that the answer from the Captain is not going to be verbal but physical. Moving very rapidly the enraged skipper catches the young man at the top of the ladder (metal stairs) and plants his big foot in a place normally used for sitting. On the way down the stairs the seaman hits every metal step with his tailbone. The Captain roars, "Get out of here, you S.O.B. and don't you ever come back. If you aren't here at 8 in the morning, I'll log (take pay away) you." The next morning promptly at 8 the seaman goes to work and nods at the Captain who just shakes his head. The Captain really likes this young lad and a day later the incident becomes a laughing matter. The young seaman, not a complete idiot, never pulls this stunt again.

<u>Kamikaze Attack</u> This story is very serious, as it involves life and death. The S.S. Jean La Fitte is in the invasion of Okinawa. The C2 ship, going in on the second wave, encounters kamikazes. A.B. Harold Knapp, is watching these incoming death planes and it looks like they are aiming right at him, so he jumps to the side. It appears that they are still aiming directly at him; so he jumps way back the other way. The kamikaze is still coming at him, but suddenly the

Gunners aim true, and the kamikaze explodes. The S.S. Jean La Fitte gets credit for 3 ½ kamikaze kills. Imagine leaning into the 20 MM machine gun aiming at an incoming kamikaze. A miss will result in the death of the Gunner and possibly the whole crew. A hit will result in the destruction of the kamikaze. A.B. Knapp presents the photos (See p 184 cc & dd) of the La Fitte. Note the airplane and three Japanese flags on the smoke stack for the three kills.

<u>Charlie Noble</u> A new first trip Ordinary Seaman on his first day at sea is sent to the wheelhouse to ask the Mate on duty if he has seen Charlie Noble. The Mate answers in the affirmative and sends the new O.S. down to the Assistant Engineer on duty in the engine room. He asks the same question and gets the same answer and is sent to the radio room. The radio officer says he has seen Charlie Noble and sends the seaman to the Chief Stewart. By now the Ordinary Seaman is beginning to realize that they are playing a game with him. It is then that someone explains to him that Charlie Noble is the galley stove pipe

<u>A Dog Named Dutch</u> While in Rotterdam, the Netherlands, an A.B. passes a pet shop and falls in love with a Brindle Boxer. The dog is only 8 weeks old, but he is huge. Captain Cook has a strict rule on his Liberty, that no pets are allowed on the ship. The A.B. can't leave without the big pup. He sneaks him onto the ship and tries to keep him hidden. Impossible! Dutch (What else would you name a dog from The Netherlands?) is eventually seen by Captain Cook. He roars," Whose dog is that?" His voice is so loud that it requires no loud speaker

S.S. JEAN LA FITTE

184 cc

S.S. JEAN LA FITTE STACK W/KILLS AND GUN TUB W/GUN

for every one on the ship to hear it. The A.B. goes to the Captain with Dutch in tow and explains that he will get the dog off the ship when the Liberty docks in Philadelphia. Eight weeks old and with a head the size of a soccer ball, Dutch immediately makes up to the Captain who says, "Okay, but when we get back –off he goes." Within several days Dutch knows his way all over the ship and his favorite place is wherever Captain Cook is. When Captain Cook whistles while on the top deck, Dutch, who is down on the stern winds his way up the various ladders to the Skipper. Then the reason for this obedience comes out. The Captain has been getting port chops, hamburger, and beef from the Chief Cook and slipping these choice treats to Dutch. By the time Philadelphia is reached the A.B. is almost afraid that he has lost his dog to Captain Cook. The A.B. ships Dutch to his parents' home and Dutch lives a long, happy life. He was always a large, gentle, lovable, and powerful dog who eventually weighs 125 pounds.

<u>Navigation</u>   Once upon a time there was a famous sea Captain. This Captain was very successful at what he did; for years he guided Merchant Ships all over the world. Never did stormy seas or pirates get the best of him. He was admired by his crew and fellow Captains. However, there was one thing different about this Captain. Every morning he went through a strange ritual. He would lock himself in his Captain's quarters and open a small safe. In the safe was an envelope with a piece of paper inside. He would stare at the paper for a minute, and then lock it back up in the safe. After this he would go about his daily duties.

For years this went on, and his crew became very curious. Was it a treasure map? Was it a letter from a long, lost love? Everyone speculated about the contents of the strange envelope. One day the Captain died at sea. After laying the Captain's body to rest, the First Mate led the entire crew into the Captain's quarters. He opened the safe, took out the envelope, opened it and the First Mate turned pale and showed the paper to the others. Four words were on the paper, two on two lines; "Port Left, Starboard Right"

Strange Reunion One of the first American vessels to be torpedoed on the Mursansk run in early 1942 was the S.S. Honomu. The Honomu's Captain, Frederick Anderson Strand, has a sister living in Norway whom he has not seen for 30 years. The Germans are very understanding and they flew Captain Strand to Oslo and arranged for a meeting between the brother and sister. A little problem is encountered in that she could not speak English and he could not speak Norwegian. Her husband, who did speak English, acted as interpreter and they had a nice visit. The captain was then transported to the German P.O.W. Camp Milag Nord (Merchant Mariners at Milag Nord Prisoners of War Camp in Germany World War II). http://www.usmm.org/milag.html

Right of Way This tale would appear to be a joke but it is true. The following is a transcript of the actual radio conversation of a U. S. Naval ship with Canadians authorities off the west coast of Newfoundland in October. 1995.

Americans: Please divert your course 15 degrees to avoid a collision.

Canadians: Recommend you divert your course 15 degrees south to avoid a collision.

Americans: This is the Captain of a U.S. Navy Ship. I say divert your course.

Canadians: No, I say again, divert your course.

Americans: This is the aircraft carrier U.S.S. Lincoln, the second largest ship in the United States Atlantic Fleet. We are accompanied by three destroyers, three cruisers and numerous support vessels. I demand that you change your course 15 degrees north, that's one five degrees north or counter measures will be undertaken for the safety of this ship.

Canadians: This is a lighthouse. Your call.. END OF MESSAGE

Pirate Story   An able bodied seaman meets a pirate in a bar, and they take turns recounting their adventures at sea. Noting the pirate's peg-leg, hook, and eye patch the seaman asks, "So, how did you end up with the peg-leg?"

The pirate replies, "We was caught in a monster storm off the cape, and a giant wave swept me overboard. Just as they was pulling me out, a school of sharks appeared and one of 'em bit me leg off."

"Blimey!" said the seaman. "What about the hook?"

"Ahhhh", mused the pirate, "we was boarding a trader ship, pistols blastin' and swords swingin' this way and that. In the fracas me hand got chopped off."

"Zounds!" remarked the seaman. "And how come ye by the eye patch?"

"A seagull droppin' fell into me eye," answered the pirate.

"You lost your eye to a seagull dropping?" the sailor asked incredulously.

"Well," said the pirate, "it was me first day with the hook....."

<u>The Friendship Ship</u> The S.S. Marshall Victory sailed from Seattle, Washington to Osaka, Japan with a cargo of wheat. This sea story is best told by 2nd Asst. Engineer John Ludwig who was there.

"Even though the war ended in 1945 the Merchant Marine was as busy in 1946 as in the war years. War weary troops were replaced with fresh troops. I sailed a trooper in November 1945 to Tokyo and Yokohama. Tokyo was a rubble! Our precision bombing had leveled the city. Saved were the Imperial Palace and grounds and the buildings to become General Eisenhower's headquarters. The Japanese accepted their defeat and gave the Americans no problems. Tokyo and Yokohama and Hiroshima and Nagasaki were fresh in my mind and I was looking forward to seeing Osaka.

What a pleasant surprise. This area had seen no hostilities. The greenery and country setting reminded me of a lush resort. Only two American soldiers were in this area. They were assigned as Provost Marshall. The town was elated to accept the American food supply. Clearly they had not expected this. In reciprocation, all ship's officers were invited to dinner. Captain's orders— Dress uniform for all men going to the dinner. We left the ship with a skeleton crew and went off to an evening of questions. Our two Army men provided transportation.

Can you imagine Hawaii in its natural state? Lush green and then a resort hotel in the center. We entered the cocktail lounge and American hard liquor was served to our order. A good start and it gets better. Our hosts were the officials and dignitaries of this area---the Governor, the Mayor, the Fire Chief, the Police Chief, the Newspaper Editor, etc. We were with the top officials. The maitre d' gave the signal and we all went upstairs. This was a ballroom and round tables seating eight were set and laden with food. The tables were about 18 inches tall. Floor pillows were our chairs. Place cards designated the seating arrangement. American, Japanese, American. We all sat, not knowing the Japanese dining procedure.

Our hosts were most gracious. Then entered the Giesha girls. A Giesha for each American. None for our hosts. What now? We soon learned to love this treatment. With chopsticks they placed food on our tongues. Served sake to our lips. What a life! Never had I had this experience before and never again. Our hosts were on their own and through signs did their best to show us a good time. After dinner we were entertained by the chalk face musicians and dancers. They played string instruments similar to a guitar. I treasure the picture taken by the News Staff.

A year ago we were enemies. Tonight we became friends. Sixty years later we are still friends" (See photo 189 ee).

The S.S. Marshall Victory returned to the U.S.A. June 1, 1946.

JAPANESE-AMERICAN DINNER 1946

Travel by Thumb   Seamen like to travel, but A.B. Jack Groethe logs many miles on both land and sea. In the early 1960's Jack decides he wants to see the world. With limited funds he takes off on a world trek—hitchhiking. He thumbs his way (not in order) through Southeast Asia, Hong Kong, Taiwan, Thailand, Burma, and Viet Nam, Nepal, Afghanistan, India, Japan, Laos, Iran, Lebanon, Jordan, Syria, Turkey, Greece, Germany, Austria, Spain, France, and the Netherlands—taking time off to run with the Bulls in Spain. His 11-month trek cost Jack just $1,100.

Jack, who left the Navy ("I wanted some sea time") for the Merchant Marine during the Viet Nam conflict, has had a varied background. He taught "conversational English" in Japan, served as a policeman, park ranger, and museum educator. Now retired, he and his wife Maggie are active in the Sons of the Union (Civil War) Veterans, where he holds the rank of Major and Historian.

Abandon Car   Sea stories can occur while traveling to catch a ship. This is a story of A.B. Edward "Ed" Dierkes, in a very strange predicament.

".....While home I ran into another seaman that I was in training with and he had a car and wanted to go to Miami, Florida, so I went with him to help drive. He was to sell the car and we were going to ship out together. (He had to get special gas ration stamps.) You couldn't find a road map those days, so we went to the Greyhound Bus Station and waited for a bus for Miami, Fl. We followed it as far as Mount Carmel, Illinois where the engine threw a rod. I had about $130 on me and he was broke, so I paid the $90 to get the car repaired. We then followed another Greyhound bus to Florida. We picked up a soldier and he directed us toward Miami. It was very late at night and we were going around a curve and all of a sudden we were airborne and splash, all this water pouring through the windows. The Soldier riding in the back seat said. " We better get out of here. People drown in this swamp when their cars go off the road." I looked at the soldier and he was between me and my buddy. I said , "How did you get up here?" He said, "I don't know." I went through the right window and I guess the soldier followed me. My buddy went out the left window (he was driving). I was swimming to the bank. He was on the trunk of the car—The car was straight up and down. When he jumped off the car he caused the car to settle on its four wheels causing the car to be completely under water. My Buddy hollered." Where's the soldier?' The soldier was on the bank and yelled, "Here I am". Back on the highway, we looked back and the headlights were still shining under the water. We were walking down the highway and a farmer came along in a pickup and picked us and took us into a small town called Everglade City. (We were very wet.) We got on a Greyhound bus and I had to pay for the soldier, my buddy, and myself. After paying for the tickets. I had less than a dollar in my pocket, but couldn't leave the soldier stranded. The driver would not let us sit because we were sopping wet. The soldier was broke, my buddy was broke, and I was broke. We got into Miami and the bus station was across the street from the Y.M.C.A.

We sat on the front steps along with a bunch of bums. It's breaking daylight and the bums were going to the docks to see if any ships came in during the night. The soldier went home, last words, "See You". We asked the bums if we could tag along. They agreed. We got to the docks and two banana boats were in and needed stevedores to unload the ship, and we went to work unloading bananas into railroad cars. We were lucky, we got paid when the ships were unloaded. The stevedores were union and when we got paid (in cash) the company deducted union dues, no social security, or payroll taxes. I wonder who really got the so-called union dues. Was this kick back? Fifty or sixty men working the docks can boil down to a lot of money in somebody's pocket. They never even wanted to know our names. There was in Miami a W.S.A. (War Shipping Administration) office. I went there and registered and reported every day that I wasn't working at the docks. We slept at a flophouse for twenty-five cents a night. One day we weren't working at the docks and were sitting around the Y.M.C.A.. Who do you think we see? The soldier. He told us that he went out to get the car and saw the car sitting at the Sheriff's Office in Everglade City and the Sheriff was looking for us. (My buddy had told the soldier that he could have the car if he could get it out of the swamp and the title was in the glove compartment.) We got on the Greyhound bus and went to Everglade City and turned ourselves in to the Sheriff. He then arrested us and put both of us in jail. My buddy was arrested for leaving the scene of an accident and other charges. I was arrested for being an accessory to the fact. A typical small southern town Sheriff, he said, "I want you boys to be my guests and spend the night with us, I'll be talking to you in the morning." The next day the Sheriff came in with a bunch of papers and said they are bills for getting the car out of the swamp, towing and dragging the swamp for bodies etc.. He would drop the charges and bills and give him $50 for the car. My buddy told the sheriff he was satisfied. We caught the next bus back to Miami. The moral is: TO HELL WITH THE BUDDY SYSTEM. I shipped alone after that."

Ed served on a number of ships including The S.S. Malay (attacked by a U-Boat) and the M.V. Marcros. The Marcros started leaking so badly that the black gang (Engine Dept.) could not keep the bilges pumped out. The Coast Guard condemned the ship as not seaworthy. The shipping company re-registered the ship under the Honduran flag (no inspections) and ordered her to sea. The Captain refused to sail and was fired. The replacement Captain got the ship to Cuba. So much water was leaking in, she was beached in Gibara, Cuba. Three months were spent in court. The no longer needed crew was flown to Miami, Fl. A.B. Dierkes discovered that seamen who know the danger of sharks had better beware of Bayou Alligators also.

CONCLUSION

In the late 1930's and early 1940's the United States has a third-rate Merchant Marine. In the light of world conditions, the United States starts up the machinery to correct this situation. Do the aggressive combatants recognize the situation the U.S.A. is in? Yes! Do they underestimate the ability of the U.S.A. to mobilize? Yes! The attack on Pearl Harbor indicates the distain the Japanese held for the U.S.

One German leader has a much better insight into the situation. When Rittmeister Monfred Von Richthoffen (80 kills), known as the Red Baron, is shot down by enemy forces in WWI.. He is succeeded by Rittmeister Rinehart, who is killed less than a month later. This casts Reichsmarshall Hermann Goring into the leadership of Von Richthofen"s "Flying Circus". He becomes a WW I hero and later rises to be the No.2 leader in Adolph Hitler's Nazi Germany.

The American Press portrays Hermann Goring in caricature fashion as a big, dumb, buffoon. This is far from the truth. Goring is a brilliant, shrewd, executive who strongly advises Adolph Hitler to keep the United States out of the war. He is very surprised when Hitler ignores his advice. Had his advice been followed and if the United States had not entered the war, history could have been much different. Can Britain prevail? Does the U.S.S.R have the power to turn the tide if Germany has to put so many troops in the west to fight the United States?

Goring fears waking up a sleeping giant and is amazed at the rate the U.S. Maritime program excelled (Photo of Goring and his fear—Liberty Ship construction (p. 195 ff). "We understood your potential. On the other hand, the tempo of your shipbuilding, for example, Henry Kaiser's program, surprised and upset us. ....At first, however, we could not believe the speed with which your Merchant Marine was growing. Claims of eight to ten days to launch a ship seemed fantastic" (World War II p. 30).

"....admitted that the Reich's leaders were shocked by the speed with which U.S. workers could produce material such as Liberty Ships, calling estimates of eight to ten days to build a ship "unthinkable" (World War II p. 29).

The shipyards under supervisors like Henry Kaiser, leading older men, farmers, and housewives (who are dubbed Rosie The Riveter), rapidly build the United States Merchant Fleet into the greatest shipping force the world has ever seen. Women enter the workplace previously dominated by men-- never to leave.

The W.S.A. (War Shipping Administration) directed by Vice Admiral Emory S. Land builds the United States Merchant Marine into a 250,000-man force that no other country can equal. The United States Maritime Service gears up three training camps that supply the men to man the rapidly growing Merchant Marine Fleet.

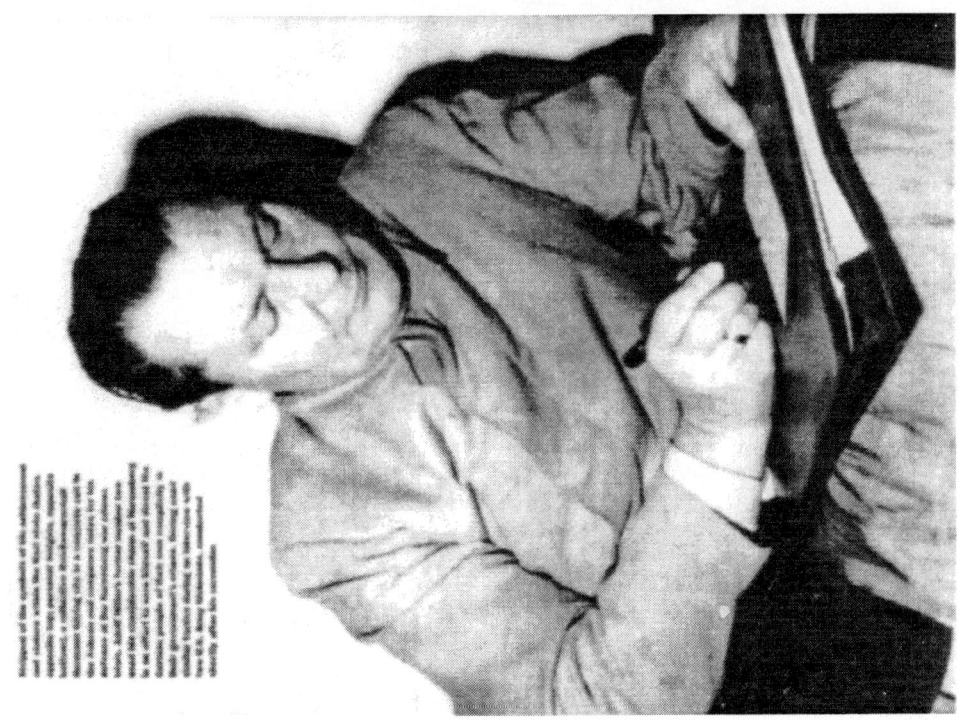

LIBERTY SHIP UNDER CONSTRUCTION

REICHSMARSHALL HERMANN GORING

195 ff

The Merchant Marine Academy at King's Point, New York takes its place along with the other military academies turning out the finest Merchant Marine Officers anywhere. This academy is the first to accept females.

The workhorse of the U.S. Merchant Marine is the "Ugly Duckling". The Liberty Ships are a vital part of every invasion. Only one ship from the thousands at the Normandy Invasion makes it back for the 50-year Anniversary and that is a Liberty—The S.S. Jeremiah O'Brien. There are still two Liberties afloat—the S.S. Jeremiah O'Brien and the S.S. John W. Brown and they are open to the public.

The WW II instructions and training seafarers receive are now under the supervision and training of the S.I.U. and excellent instruction is given. A seafarer can also earn a college degree at Piney Point, Maryland.

The Navy Armed Guard Seamen suffer losses along with the Z-Men. They suffer one of the largest percentages of losses of any unit in the Navy. Today they have their own veterans' organization. Quite a few Gunners also belong to Merchant Marine Veteran groups. Sailors and Seamen live and work on the same ship, go on pass together, fight the enemy together and all too often die together. They "deliver the goods" together. The Naval Armed Guard has long been disbanded, but they will be long remembered.

For the person interested in Merchant Ships, The U.S. Government Printing Office published "Ships of the Merchant Marine" in 1950. There are 20 ships listed with dimensions, draft, tonnage, engine etc. There are pictures of the ships, plus miscellaneous photos in this 21-page booklet.

The U.S. Merchant Marine motto is "We deliver the goods". The goods are delivered in WW II --270 million tons of cargo and billions of gallons of gasoline and oil. This amounted to 4,000 tons <u>every hour of every day</u>. Ten million men are transported to the war and back home after the war. The war actually lasted 1,364 days, 5 hours and 14 minutes. President George W. Bush said in his 2005 National Maritime Day speech that the Merchant Marine moves more than 2 billion tons of domestic and international freight into the U.S. each year.

The Z-Men do not receive veteran status until 1988, and those who do not board a ship until after August 15, 1945 have to wait another 10 years until 1998 to receive their veteran status. During this 53 year wait the majority of the Mariners has "crossed over the bar".

The men who train the troops in the United States Maritime Service have never received veterans' status. These men who are former seamen, and former Navy and Coast Guard sailors wear USMS uniforms and receive the same pay as soldiers and other servicemen. There are only a few left, but they are still waiting and hoping for recognition.

The Z-Men who waited so long for veterans' status and never received the G I Bill or V A benefits are now hopeful that a so-called "Belated Thank You" bill will pass. Senate Bill 1272 and House of Representatives Bill 23 would give each WW II Z-Man $1,000 per month to make up for what they did not receive after WW II. When the bills were introduced, Congress estimated that approximately 10.000 seamen were still alive out of 250,000. In the two years that have elapsed the figure is now approximately 8,000.

The future of the U.S. Merchant Marine is bright. More modern ships are being built. The Merchant Mariners today are very much involved. The cadets and seafarers are active immediately following the 9-11 tragedies. The flooding disasters in Louisiana sees mariners move in to lend assistance. In fact one Merchant Ship is still there. This ship is keeping medications and essential items refrigerated while electrical power is down in that area. Tom Casey, who is now qualified for a Captain's license, was Chief Mate on that vessel until late July 2006. See Captain Casey assisting St. Louis Port Agent Becky Sleeper (seafarer) putting up a Merchant Marine Flag in the S.I.U. Hall in St. Louis, Mo. (p.198 gg).

This study has concentrated on the U.S. Merchant Marine with special emphasis on the Liberty Ship and the Z-Men. For those interested in a broader view of the USMM in and after WW II that includes all types of ships, Captain Arthur R. Moore has a new 8th Edition of his <u>A Careless Word ...A Needless Sinking</u> that is just released in August 2006. This reference covers all catastrophic ship losses not just the Liberty Ships. His research includes U.S. documents, statements from survivors, the Oil and the Freight Company's records

ST. LOUIS PORT AGENT BECKY SLEEPER (SEAFARER)
AND CAPTAIN TOM CASEY

ANCHOR MONUMENT
WITH USMM FLAG

USMM, US, ARMED GUARD FLAGS, 1998
VETERANS' DAY PARADE, ST. LOUIS, MO

USMM FLAGS WITH USMM SEAFARERS

A careless word...
A history of the tremendous losses in ships and men suffered by the U.S. Merchant Marine during World War II 1941-1945
Capt. Arthur R. Moore
...A NEEDLESS SINKING

and many other resources. He also covers the fate of the 500 American Z-Men lost on foreign flag ships. This book is highly recommended as the best WW II USMM reference available. See Captain Moore's poster (p.199 hh).

It is correct to say that the United States won WW II. It is a victory, yes, but at what a price? Thousands of people are killed including non-combatants killed by bombs. There are many with injuries (thousands permanent), disrupted lives, etc. etc. Superintendent Ralph Weichert (Soldiers' Memorial, St. Louis, Mo.) sums it up for the Merchant Marine when he says, "There are no tombstones on the sea—only the drifting remnants of disaster. The ocean floor is littered with the skeletons of ships and sailors who died that freedom might live. The waste and wreckage of war clutters mile on mile of the silent deep—dead ships---dead sailors (Weichert--5/22/01).

If there is a dad or a granddad or someone else who was a seaman, just ask, " What its the latest scuttlebutt (gossip)?" Or "Have you ever been hit by a monkey fist?" (Knotted ball on the end of a heaving line). There is sure to be a smile. There may even be a sea story or two. You may learn of the time in Calcutta, India, when he and two shipmates rented three rickshaws, put the coolies (pullers) in the rickshaws and then they pulled them to see who was the strongest and fastest for a block or so. If grandma is not around you may hear about a pretty lass he took dancing in Liverpool, England. He may talk about the dark haired beauty from Naples, Italy that he trudged up Mt . Vesuvius with. If, by chance, he was on one of the 733 ships (229 Liberties) that were sunk by enemy action he might even tell you how on the order to "abandon ship" he jumped with only the clothes on his back and a life jacket thirty feet into burning oil. How he was lucky enough to make it to a lifeboat or a life raft and then spent seven or more hot days and cold nights praying as he never prayed before that a U.S. or Allied Ship would pick them up. If he tends to ramble a little, overlook it because at his age he is soon to "cross over the bar" (die). However do not pity him. He has gone where few men dared to go, seen things and had thrills that few men ever experience and still had over 60 years to savor the memories. Always remember the old guy is not just a man--- he is a **Z-Man!**

BIBLIOGRAPHY

Allsup, Dan "We Deliver The Goods" <u>The American Legion Magazine</u> SEPT. 2005

American Merchant Marine Men And Ships In WWII

    Retrieved From World-Wide Web 1998

    http://w.w.w.usmm.org

American Merchant Marine Casualties

    Retrieved From World-Wide Web 6/27/2006

    http://www.usmm.org/casualty.html

American Merchant Marine P.O.W's and M.I.A.'s

    Retrieved From World-Wide Web 6/27/2006

    http://www.usmm.org./duffy.html

Army Releases Former Mariners For Sea Duty

    Retrieved From World-Wide Web 3/21/05

    www.net army release.html

Boattalk Nautical Dictionary

    Retrieved From World-Wide Web 11/30/2005

    www.boattalk.com/dictionary/index.htm

Capt Warren G Leback   What Did Your Liberty Ship Cost?

    S.S.Samuel Parker Chapter, Box 20107. St. Louis, Mo. 63123-0307

    Newsletter April 15, 1999

Chronology of U.S. Merchant Marine Struggle for Recognition and Justice

    Retrieved From World-Wide Web 2/22/2005

    http://www.usmm.org

Cigarette Sinks A Ship

    Retrieved From World-Wide Web 7/10/2006

    http://www.usmm.net/cigarette.html

Cornell, Felix M and Hoffman, Allan C <u>American Merchant Seaman"s Manual</u>

    Cornell Maritime Press New York 1942

Dierkes, Edward G. Captain S.S. Samuel Parker Chapter St. Louis Mo.

    Speech 5/22/2006

Dooley, Francis J. Letter to Congress of the United States <u>American Merchant Marine Veterans News</u>

    Spring 2006

Farrar, Frank F. Capt, (1988) <u>A Ships Log Book</u>

    Great Outdoors Publishing Co. St. Petersburg. Fl. 33714 1988

Floating Tombstones

    Retreived from the World-Wide Web 4/25/2006

    http://ummusem.mus.pa.us/concrete.htm

Gallant Ships of WW II Merchant Marine

    Retrieved from the World-Wide Web 2/2/006

    http://www.usmm.org/gallant ships.html

History Of The Draft

    Retrieved from the World-Wide Web 11/23/2005

    en.wikipedia.org/wiki/Selective_Service_Act

Hope. Bob, "Christmas 1944 Broadcast To U.S. Merchant Marine Everywhere"

    Midwest Chapter American Merchant Marine Newsletter Fall 1999

Jaffee, W.W. Capt. (2004) S.S. Jeremiah O' Brien

    The Glencannon Press Palo Alto, Ca 2004

Jaffee, Walter W., The Last Liberty

    The Glencannon Press Palo Alto, Ca 1993

Jaffee. Walter W. The Liberty Ships From A to Z

    The Glencannon Press Palo Alto, Ca 2004

Last Of The Liberty Ships

    Retrieved From The World-Wide Web   4/21/2006

    http:www.cascobay.com/history/libship/libship.htm

Ludwig, John First Assistant Engineer, Retired St. Louis, Mo.

    Correspondence 7/7/06

Maritime American Merchant Marine Veterans

    Produced by the S.S. Stephen Hopkins Chapter 2006

Merchant Marine at Milog Nord Prisoner of War Camp in Germany World War II

    Retrieved From The World-Wide Web 7/10/2006

    http://www.usmm.org/milog.html

Mc Combs, Don and Worth, Fred L. World War II Strange and Fascinating Facts

    Greenwich House Distributed by Crown Publishers, Inc New York 1983

Merchant Marine Emblems, Medals and Ribbons

    Retrieved From The World-Wide Web 2/2/2006

    http://wwwusmm.org/medals.html

Monthly Pay Scale For Liberty Vessels

    S.S. Samuel Parker Chapter. Box 20107, St Louis, Mo.63123-0307

    Newsletter May 14, 2001

Moore, Arthur R., Capt. A Carless Word...A Needless Sinking Eighth Edition

    American Merchant Marine Museum 2006

National Maritime Day Proclamation 2005 by President of The United States of America—George W. Bush 2005

Paul Hall Center For Maritime Training And Education

    Catalog 2006-2007 Piney Point Md 20674-0075

Project Liberty Ship

    Retrieved From The World-Wide Web 5/4//2006

    http://www.libertyships.com/html/brown

Reminick, Gerald, <u>Nightmare In Bari</u>

    The Glencannon Press Palo, Ca. 2001

Reminick, Gerald, <u>Patriots And Heroes</u>

    The Glencannon Press Palo, Ca. 2000

Rexford, Peter A Ship May Soon Come For Overlooked War Veterans

    St Louis Dispatch 7/17/06

St Louis Anchor Dedication, Michael Sacco Speech

    St. Louis, Mo. July 5, 1999

Sacco, Michael, President's Report

    S.I.U. Seafarers Log April 2006

Sawyer, L.A. and Mitchell W.H. (1995) <u>The Liberty Ships, Second Edition</u>

    Lloyd's of London Press Ltd San Francisco 1985

<u>Ship Losses In Gulf Of Mexico During WWII</u>

    Jurgen Rohwer, Axis Submarine Successes 1939-1945

Ships Of The American Merchant Marine At War

    United States Maritime Commission 1950

    U.S Government Printing Office 1950

SIU: We Could Not Have Fought This War Without You

    Retrieved From World- Web 4/18/2006

    www.seafarers.org/log/2006/042006/mtdoif.xml

S.S. Jeremiah O'Brien Liberty Ship

    Sixth Annual Seamen"s Memorial Cruise

    May 18. 1985

<u>The Liberty Ships of World War II</u> (S.S. Robert E. Peary)

U.S. Armed Guard, 5712 Partridge Lane, Raleigh, N.C. 27609- 4126

    August 1998

The Mighty Liberties

    S.S. Samuel Parker Chapter, Box 20107, St. Louis, Mo.63123-0307

    Newsletter January 1, 2006

<u>The U.S. Merchant Marine</u> Turner Publisher Turner Publishing Co

    Paculah, Ky 42101 1993

The United States Merchant Marine At War

    U.S. Government Printing Office

    January 15, 1946

Top Secret Project Ivory Soap—Aircraft Repair Ships

    Retrieved from the World-Wide Web 7/10/2006

    http://www.usmm.org/felknerivory.html

Torpedoed Four Times During World War II

    Retrieved from the World-Wide Web 7/10/2006

    http://www.usmm.org/lopez.html

U.S. Maritime Service—The Forgotten Service

    Retrieved from the World-Wide Web February 2, 2006

    www.usmm.org/usms.html February 2, 2006

U.S. Maritime Service To Accept 16 Year Olds For Training

    Retrieved From World-Wide Web 4/20/2006

    http://www.usmm.net/16yearold.html

<u>U.S Merchant Marine</u>

    Turner Publishing Co. Padulah, Ky 42101 1993

War Shipping Administration. Established by President Franklin Delano

    Roosevelt Executive Order No. 9054 February 7, 1942

    http;//www.org/fdr/wsa/law.html 4/20/06

Weichert, Ralph Superintendent Soldiers Memorial, St. Louis, Mo.

    Speech May 22, 2001

World War II "The Reichsmarshall's Revelations"

    Interviewed by Major Kenneth W. Hechler U.S. Army 7/25/45

Young, Burt Should Veteran Status Be Dependent On A Kangaroo Court?

Dageforde Publishing, Inc Crete, Ne 68333   2003

APPENDICES

Liberty Ship Profile………………………………………………	6a
Liberty Ship Jeremiah O'Brien…………………………………….	27b
USMS Emblem, USMS Trainee, USMS Trainees……………..	32c
St Catherine Hotel, Casino……………………………………….	34d
Coast Guard Certificate of Service Etc.…………………………….	36e.f.g
Ship Loses in Gulf of Mexico,…………………………………….	41h
Merchant Vessels Attacked in Gulf, German U-Boats…………….	41i
Working High, Wheel House……………………………………..	53j
Whistle and Knife………………………………………………..	113k
Ship Discharges…………………………………………………..	118l
Citations…………………………………………………………..	119m
Uncle Sam Poster…………………………………………………	132n
Recruitment Posters………………………………………………	132o
Lifeboat……………………………………………………………	158p
You Bet Poster……………………………………………………	159q
Some Day Poster…………………………………………………	160r
Honorable Discharge……………………………………………...	161s
Jefferson Barracks Monument……………………………………	165t
Anchor at Soldiers' Memorial……………………………………	166u
Merchant Marine Anthem……………………………………….	166v
Merchant Marine Anthem Continued……………………………	166w
S.S. Samuel Parker………………………………………………	167x

USMM Medals and Decorations...168y

Commemorative Medals...169z

S.S. Jeremiah O'Brien..177aa

S.S. John W. Brown...178bb

S.S. Jean LaFitte..184cc

S.S. Jean LaFitte Stack with Kills and Gun Tub with Gun 184dd

Japanese-American Dinner 1946..189ee

Reichsmarshall Goering and Liberty Ship Construction.........................195ff

USMM Flags with USMM Seafarers...198gg

Slip of the Lip Poster..199hh

DR. GEORGE E. WARD, JR.
IS ONE OF THE REMAINING 3% WWII Z-MEN.
HE SERVED IN ALL THE WAR ZONES ON
FOUR DIFFERENT LIBERTIES AND IN
17 FOREIGN COUNTRIES.

ISBN 1425119824

9 781425 119829